10,000 COMEDIANS

the no BS! Tour

Screenplay by,

Harry Lee

Howlin' Wolf Studio™
www.howlinwolfstudio.com

ISBN: 979-8-9878457-6-9 (sc)
ISBN: 979-8-9878457-5-2 (hc)
ISBN: 979-8-9878457-7-6 (e)

Library of Congress Control Number: 2023921914

The views of the author expressed in this book are solely those of the author, and the publisher disclaims any responsibility for the author's interpretation of events.

Cover Image: Used Under License – dan.nikonov/Shutterstock.com

FADE IN:

OVER OPENING CREDITS:

1   INT. TARGET RESIDENCE - NIGHT

Dim illumination from night lights that are plugged into
electrical outlets low on the wall shows someone WALKING
along a darkened hallway. The person approaches a set of
stairs and DESCENDS. The ground floor is also darkened except
for more night lights at low wall outlets. The person turns a
corner and enters the kitchen, the only illumination coming
from the over-the-stove hood light. In the semi-darkness is
exposed a sloppy kitchen in this apparently upscale home.
Seen in the sink is a pile of dirty dishes and open food
packaging is scattered on the countertop. The person goes to
the refrigerator and opens the door. The light comes on and
the person leans forward, reaching into the refrigerator.
Fully exposed in the light from the refrigerator is seen a
FIRST MAN who appears to be Hispanic, his unshaven face
showing dark whiskers. At the end of a tattooed arm is an
expensive gold wristwatch. With his fingers he grabs the
necks of three bottles of beer. The first man closes the
door, turns and walks back the way he came, up the staircase
to the second floor.

2   INT. TARGET RESIDENCE - 2ND FLOOR HALLWAY - CONTINUOUS

The first man approaches and opens a door, light spills out
into the hallway. He enters the room, closing the door behind
him.

3   INT. TARGET RESIDENCE - SECOND FLOOR BEDROOM - CONTINUOUS

Inside the brightly lit room are TWO MEN and TWO WOMEN. These
two men and two women are wearing latex surgical gloves on
their hands. Like the first man, the other two men and two
women are also Hispanic and of the same age which appears to
be twenty to forty. The WINDOW in the room is HEAVILY
CURTAINED, blocking all light and view from inside and
outside. The first man hands a beer to each of the two men.

(SUBTITLES IN ENGLISH)

                    1ST OF TWO MEN
          Contar dinero es un trabajo
          sediento. (Counting money is
          thirsty work.)

The others laugh. The first man reaches out to a ceramic dish on the table, he uses the manicured long fingernail on his pinky finger to scoop up some WHITE POWDER which he raises to his nose and SNORTS.

This room in the home is a bedroom but the normal furniture has been replaced by tables along two adjoining walls. The two men are sitting in chairs at the tables. One table is stacked with LOOSE CURRENCY, that one man and one woman are sorting by denomination and turning face up. They place the organized stacks onto the neighboring table where the other man feeds the bills into a HI-SPEED CASH COUNTING MACHINE. The second woman takes the neatly stacked and counted bills and puts a BANKERS BAND on them. She sets the banded stack at the end of the table. The first man makes a slash mark on a pad of paper, tabulating the count of stacks, then puts the banded cash into a CARDBOARD OFFICE STYLE STORAGE BOX. Leaning against the wall and on the tables are multiple firearms, PISTOLS, REVOLVERS, and ASSAULT RIFLES. The other wall is stacked with more banker boxes, sealed with packing tape and stacked in an orderly arrangement from the floor to the ceiling. Pan to CLOSE ON the hi-speed counting machine. A hand places a stack of one-hundred dollar bills into the machine feeder. A finger pushes a button on the machine. The image blurs as the bills are rapidly shuffled and professionally counted.

END OPENING CREDITS:

4   I/E. MONTANA'S TRUCK - CITY STREET - MORNING

Through the windshield of a MOVING VEHICLE is seen a multi-lane roadway with commercial establishments each side of the street. There is some light city traffic. On top of the dashboard is a pile of folded maps, sunglasses, and a few cassette tapes. Ahead, a traffic light is approached that turns to RED. The vehicle stops. Still from the view inside the vehicle are seen STREET SIGNS showing this is the intersection of HOLLYWOOD BOULEVARD and VINE STREET. The light turns GREEN, the vehicle rolls forward.

5   INT. HOLLYWOOD BOULEVARD - RESTAURANT - MOMENTS LATER

The front of the restaurant faces Hollywood Boulevard with plate glass windows allowing a view of the sidewalk and street of this world famous district in the city of Los Angeles. The manager, BOB, is middle-aged, dressed in dark slacks, white shirt and dark tie. A waitress, SHIRLEY, not old but not young, a veteran of the Hollywood scene, is dressed in a waitress uniform with an apron tied around her waist. They are standing by the cash register talking.

                    SHIRLEY/WAITRESS
          The jerk didn't leave me a tip. Can
          you believe it? I don't ever want
          to wait on him again. I see him
          come in, I'm going on break.

                    BOB/MANAGER
          Maybe he just overlooked it. I hear
          he's working on a difficult shoot.
          You know, got a lot on his mind.

                    SHIRLEY/WAITRESS
          I don't care if he is a big shot
          director. That's no reason to be
          rude.

The manager is looking out the window and sees a pickup truck
pull up and park on the street right in front. The truck
passenger door is painted with a cowboy riding a rearing
bull, a set of long bull horns are bolted on the engine hood
and the truck has a large slide-in camper on the back. The
whole apparatus is well used, dusty as if its traveled many
miles.

                    BOB/MANAGER
          You don't see a setup like that
          every day.

Shirley turns and sees a man get out of the truck driver's
door and walk around the front of the truck to the sidewalk.
He has a slight but noticeable limp. He's a slim, late-20's
man dressed casually in jeans, cowboy boots, a pearl-button
style cowboy shirt and cowboy hat.

                    SHIRLEY/WAITRESS
          Oh, great. The cowboys are always
          big tippers.

                    BOB/MANAGER
          Maybe he's a rich oil man, like
          J.R. Maybe he'll sweep you off your
          feet, Shirley, and take you out of
          here.

                    SHIRLEY/WAITRESS
          Yeah, right. Only in the movies.

The door opens and the cowboy enters the restaurant. This is
MONTANA. He has in his hand a rolled up magazine.

                    MONTANA
               (a country accent)
          Well, I be dawg! Here I am on
          Hollywood Boulevard.
                    (MORE)

                    MONTANA (CONT'D)
          Can you believe it? Hello folks. My
          name's Jimmy but everybody calls me
          Montana. I just got in town. This
          is going to be my first meal in
          Hollywood.

Montana steps to the counter, swings his right leg over the
stool like he's mounting a horse and sits.

                    BOB/MANAGER
          Welcome to Hollywood, Montana.
          Would you care for breakfast?

                    MONTANA
          That sounds mighty fine. I hope you
          got a steer on the spit because I'm
          plumb starved.

Shirley places a menu on the counter.

                    SHIRLEY/WAITRESS
          Are you from Montana? Is that why
          they call you Montana?

                    MONTANA
          Oh, no, ma'am. A dern bull named
          Montana busted my hip in Montana.
          That's why they call me Montana.
          I'm from West Virginia, originally.

                    SHIRLEY/WAITRESS
          A bull? Uh, huh. Would you like
          coffee?

                    MONTANA
          Well, sure. Coffee'd be mighty
          fine.

Shirley, at the coffee machine, in a low voice to Bob.

                    SHIRLEY/WAITRESS
          Ma'am! He called me ma'am. Do I
          look like a freaking ma'am?

                    BOB/MANAGER
          He's just being polite, Shirley.
          All cowboys are polite. You've seen
          them in the movies, they're always
          polite to the women folks.

Bob turns back to the counter.

                    BOB/MANAGER (CONT'D)
          Montana, this is Shirley, and my
          name's Bob.
                    (tries on a country
                     accent)
          It's mighty fine this here is your
          first stop.
                    (back to normal voice)
          Relax. Make yourself at home, and
          Shirley will get you taken care of.

                    MONTANA
          I'm mighty pleased to meet you,
          Shirley and, Bob. I appreciate the
          hospitality.

Setting down the coffee cup and small containers.

                    SHIRLEY/WAITRESS
          Here's the cream and sugar if you
          want it.

                    MONTANA
                    (pointing at menu)
          Okie, dokie. I'll take this here
          Big Breakfast. The picture looks
          mighty fine.

                    SHIRLEY/WAITRESS
          Big Breakfast. Mighty fine! Okie,
          dokie.

Bob goes through the swinging kitchen door. Shirley follows
with the order. Montana sips the coffee, then unrolls the
magazine. We see it's *The Hollywood Reporter.*

Shirley comes back through the kitchen door.

                    SHIRLEY/WAITRESS (CONT'D)
          So, you're from West Virginia? I've
          never been there. What's it like?

                    MONTANA
          It's mostly coal mines and hills
          and forests, called the Mountain
          State, because it's the only state
          completely in the Appalachian
          mountains. I grew up in a little
          place called "No Holler."

                    SHIRLEY/WAITRESS
          That's a funny name. Why is it
          called No Holler?

                    MONTANA
Because the holler's so small, when
you holler, you don't get a holler
echo back at ya.

                    SHIRLEY/WAITRESS
Uh, huh. So how did you get to
Montana from No Holler?

                    MONTANA
I'm a rodeo'er.
        (stands and points to his
         large belt buckle, then
         sits)
I'm a bull rider. I won this here
buckle at the National Finals. I've
been rodeo'in about five years
now.

                    SHIRLEY/WAITRESS
Is there a rodeo in LA?

                    MONTANA
Oh, no, ma'am - I mean, Shirley. I
had to give it up. Last July that
dern bull busted my hip, at the
Last Chance Stampede Rodeo in
Helena, Montana. I've been laid up
the last two months. Now I'm
changing careers.

                    SHIRLEY/WAITRESS
What are you going to do now?

                    MONTANA
I've come to Hollywood to be a
movie star! I need an agent. You
know any agents?

                    SHIRLEY/WAITRESS
A movie star? Okie, dokie!

Bob comes in from the swinging kitchen door.

                    SHIRLEY/WAITRESS (CONT'D)
Bob, Montana is going to be a movie
star. He's looking for an agent.
Who do you recommend?

                    BOB/MANAGER
There's a lady comes in for lunch,
she's an agent. Her name is Nicole.
                    (MORE)

                    BOB/MANAGER (CONT'D)
          Her office is right down the
          street. I'll write down the address
          for you.

Bob goes back to the kitchen.

                    MONTANA
          Well, I be dawg! Coming in here and
          meeting ya'll is what's called a
          serendipitous encounter! I'll get
          my star out there on the sidewalk
          before ya know it! Have you seen
          that walk of fame, Shirley? That's
          something ain't it!

                    SHIRLEY/WAITRESS
          Montana, this is a tough town and
          acting is a tough act to break
          into. I've done some acting, in
          front of the camera, and on stage.
          It's hard to get that lucky break,
          to make a career out of it.

                    MONTANA
          Well, sure. I figured that. I'm
          gonna give it a shot, though. I
          figure if Festus can be a movie
          star, then so can I.

                    SHIRLEY/WAITRESS
          Festus?

                    MONTANA
          Festus! Yeah, you know, the TV
          show, the western, Gunsmoke. Festus
          had a limp and talked kinda funny,
          but he's a movie star. I watch the
          reruns every chance I get.

                    SHIRLEY/WAITRESS
          Festus? Okie, dokie!

DING. DING. The bell at the kitchen serve-thru window rings,
indicating the order is up. Shirley turns to get the food.
She sets the plates in front of Montana. Montana shakes salt
and pepper on the food -- then he jerks back in horror!

                    MONTANA
              AHHH!

Montana slides the plate down the counter, away from him. Bob
is nearby and immediately comes over.

                    BOB/MANAGER
          Something wrong, Montana?

                    MONTANA
               (jerks a thumb toward the
                plate)
          Thar's a fur-burger hare on my
          biscuit!

                    BOB/MANAGER
               (uncomprehendingly)
          What?

                    MONTANA
               (pointing)
          Thar's a fur-burger hare on my
          biscuit. See? Right thar!

Bob looks closer. ZOOM on BISCUIT. Sure enough, there's a
HAIR on the biscuit. Bob is mortified.

                    BOB/MANAGER
          Oh, my god!
               (grabs the plate)
          I'm very sorry, Montana. We'll get
          you a new breakfast, right away. On
          the house. Sit tight.

Bob goes into the kitchen through the swinging door.

                    MONTANA
               (talking to himself)
          The only thing worse than a fur-
          burger hare on the biscuit is a
          roach swimming in the soup!

6   INT. RESTAURANT - KITCHEN - CONTINUOUS

Bob, standing by the grill, is talking to the cook, CECIL.
Cecil is a Black older gentleman, a professional chef.

                    BOB/MANAGER
               (mimicking Montana's
                accent)
          Cecil, thar's a fur-burger hare on
          the biscuit!

Cecil is in his white chef's uniform with a chef's cap. Cecil
looks at Bob, uncomprehendingly.

                    CECIL
          Say what?

Bob points to the biscuit.

>   BOB/MANAGER
>   Looky thar! Right thar! A fur-
>   burger hare!

Now Cecil sees the hair on the biscuit. Cecil grabs the plate. Cecil tosses the whole she-bang, plate and all, into the trash can. Bob walks away. Cecil cracks new eggs on the grill.

>   CECIL
>   (mockingly mimics accent)
>   *Fur-burger hare!*

Cecil looks over his shoulder, and tells an ASSISTANT:

>   CECIL (CONT'D)
>   Check the biscuits! Make sure...
>   *thar's no fur-burger hare on the*
>   *biscuits*!

7   INT. RESTAURANT - MOMENTS LATER

Montana is engrossed in reading the paper. DING. DING. The bell at the kitchen serve-thru window rings, indicating the order is up. Shirley sets the plate in front of Montana.

>   SHIRLEY/WAITRESS
>   Sorry about that, Montana. That's
>   the first time its happened.

8   INT. RESTAURANT - KITCHEN - MOMENTS LATER

From an OVERHEAD VIEW - two hands in restaurant-grade stainless steel mesh protective gloves are at the end of two white sleeves. One of the hands has a bloody cleaver clenched firmly. The hands are busily and efficiently chopping up a large piece of meat into soup-sized bits. WHACK, the cleaver smacks the meat. WHACK. RED BLOOD is smeared on the cleaver and the white prep tabletop. WHACK. The process becomes more intense. WHACK. WHACK. Now we HEAR Cecil, but only SEE his hands:

>   CECIL (V.O.)
>   (grumbling, mimicking)
>   *Fur burger hare on the biscuit!*

HANDS CHOPPING. WHACK. WHACK.

>   CECIL (V.O.)
>   Come in here...

HANDS CHOPPING. WHACK, WHACK.

                    CECIL (V.O.)
          Talking that honky hillbilly
          sounding bullshit.

HANDS CHOPPING, QUICKER. WHACK. WHACK. WHACK. WHACK.

CLOSE UP on Cecil's face: he looks very agitated.

                    CECIL
          That peckerwood hillbilly
          muthafu...!

                                        CUT TO:

9   INT. RESTAURANT - CONTINUOUS

Montana is at the cash register with Shirley and Bob.

                    BOB/MANAGER
          No, it's on the house, Montana. I'm
          sorry about that. It's like a
          cliché - a hair on a biscuit. It's
          the first time I've actually ever
          seen it in all the years I've been
          in the business.

                    MONTANA
          I told ya it's not necessary,
          picking up the check, but what the
          heck, thank ye much.
               (hands Shirley a bill)
          Here, Shirley, you take that.

Shirley looks at it:

                    SHIRLEY/WAITRESS
          This is a one-hundred dollar bill!
          I can't take that. It's too much.

                    MONTANA
          Never argue with the customer! Put
          that in your pocket. It was worth
          every nickel. Meeting you fine
          folks, enjoying your company, the
          fine meal.

                    SHIRLEY/WAITRESS
          You just got in town. Can you
          afford this?

                    MONTANA
          Shoot. You kidding? I stopped off
          in Vegas on the way here. Played
          some poker, got some traveling
          money. Everything's fine and dandy.

                    SHIRLEY/WAITRESS
          You win? Playing poker? In Vegas?

                    MONTANA
          Well, sure. Those ole boys that
          hang out at the casinos, they just
          give their money away.

                    SHIRLEY/WAITRESS
          What do you mean?

                    MONTANA
          Those guys aren't there to win,
          they're just there to play. They
          have to play. Win, lose, or draw,
          doesn't matter, they just have to
          play. The psychiatrists call it a
          gambling disorder, or some such
          thing.

                    SHIRLEY/WAITRESS
          You win!?

                    MONTANA
          Yep. Those ole boys couldn't bluff
          their way out of a wet paper sack.
          Well, I'm on my way to see Nicole
          about being my agent. I'll let ya
          know how it goes.

     Montana turns toward the door.

                                             CUT TO:

10   INT. RESTAURANT - KITCHEN - CONTINUOUS

     FACING the kitchen side of the metal swinging door as it is
     VIOLENTLY KICKED open. BANG. The door smashes into the wall
     leading into the restaurant.

                                             CUT TO:

11   INT. RESTAURANT - CONTINUOUS

     At the sudden BANG of the door opening, Montana, Shirley, and
     Bob, all jerk around to see Cecil standing in the doorway.

He has on his white prep jacket, the front smeared with red blood from the meat chopping work. His stainless-steel gloved hand at the end of the white sleeved arm has the BLOODY CLEAVER clenched, pointing directly at Montana.

                    CECIL
          Hey, you! Cowboy!

Montana looks at Cecil in astonishment.

                    MONTANA
               (taps a finger on his
                chest)
          Me?

                    CECIL
               (demanding, challenging)
          Who's Charlie Pride?

                    MONTANA
          What? Everybody knows Charlie
          Pride! He's the best country
          western singer in the whole wide
          world.

Cecil slowly lowers the cleaver. Cecil looks at Bob the manager, who is staring at Cecil.

                    CECIL
          Alright. Alright. The cowboy's
          alright with me.

Cecil turns and goes back into the kitchen. Shirley, Bob, and Montana stand looking at one another.

                    MONTANA
          Well, okie dokie! See ya'll later.

Montana goes out the door. Some customers set still and quiet, looking at the kitchen door the obviously crazed man in the white chef's uniform and bloody cleaver in his hand had just gone through.

                    BOB/MANAGER
               (makes a joke of it)
          We're rehearsing for a Halloween
          movie folks. It's all just for fun.

A TOURIST MAN and a TOURIST WOMAN at a table suddenly laugh.

                    TOURIST WOMAN
          Isn't this wonderful, honey?
          Hollywood. I love it!

12   EXT. HOLLYWOOD BOULEVARD - CONTINUOUS

Montana's truck pulls out and drives away.

13   INT. RESTAURANT - CONTINUOUS

Shirley and Bob are standing by the cash register, looking
out the window, watching Montana's truck driving away on
Hollywood Boulevard.

                    BOB/MANAGER
          That was an interesting start to
          the day.

                    SHIRLEY/WAITRESS
               (looking at the $100
                dollar bill)
          Yep. It was mighty fine!

                                        DISSOLVE TO:

14   EXT. HOLLYWOOD BOULEVARD - LATER

Montana is walking on the sidewalk. He checks a piece of
paper in his hand, checks the address of the building he
stops in front of, opens the door and enters the lobby.

15   INT. NICOLE, THE AGENT - RECEPTION AREA - MOMENTS LATER

The door opens and Montana enters. In a rectangular room, at
a desk, sits the receptionist, SALLY. The wall behind Sally
has a door leading to inner offices, the wall also has a
collection of movie posters and framed photos. Along the
other two walls, sitting in adjacent chairs, are a half-dozen
or so ACTORS waiting their turn to go in for the audition.

                    MONTANA
          Hello! I'm an actor, and here to
          see Ms. Nicole, the agent.

                    SALLY/RECEPTIONIST
               (looks at a paper)
          What's your name?

                    MONTANA
          My name's Jimmy Kennedy Garrett.
          But you can call me, Montana.
          Everybody calls me, Montana.

> SALLY/RECEPTIONIST
> I don't see your name on the list,
> Mr. Garrett, ah, Mr. Montana. Are
> you here for the audition?

> MONTANA
> What's your name, ma'am?

> SALLY/RECEPTIONIST
> I'm Sally, Mrs. Franklin's
> receptionist.

> MONTANA
> Well, howdy, Sally. I'm pleased to
> make your acquaintance. Please,
> just call me Montana. I was told
> that I should see Mrs. Nicole.
> Here's my resume.
>> (hands Sally a sheet of
>> paper)
> If you could put my name on the
> list it would sure be appreciated.

> SALLY/RECEPTIONIST
>> (copying from resume)
> I can add you at the end. Please
> have a seat.

Sally takes Montana's resume through the door to the inner
office, returning in just seconds. Montana sits in a seat,
nodding politely to the people on each side of him. He looks
around at the other actors who are waiting. They each are
reading from a sheet of paper and seem to be having a silent
conversation with an invisible person, their lips moving, but
silent, exercising their facial muscles in various
expressions of happiness, sadness, surprise, contempt and
other private thoughts.

> SALLY/RECEPTIONIST (CONT'D)
> Mr. Montana, do you have a sides?

> MONTANA
> A sides of what?

> SALLY/RECEPTIONIST
>> (shows a sheet of paper)
> The audition sides. The monologue.

> MONTANA
> No, I sure don't.

Montana rises, steps to the desk and takes the paper.

                         MONTANA (CONT'D)
                    Well, thank ye much!

Montana sits and studies the sheet of paper. He looks at the
other people who are reading the sides and having a silent
conversation with themselves.

                         MONTANA (CONT'D)
                      (smiles, whispers)
                    Ahh! Okie dokie.

Montana begins to read the sides and, like the others, begins
to have a quiet private conversation with himself. His facial
expressions are exaggerated.

                                        DISSOLVE TO:

16   INT. NICOLE, THE AGENT - RECEPTION AREA - LATER

Montana is the last actor waiting. The door behind Sally's
desk opens and a MAN/ACTOR comes into the room. The man is
breathing fast, as if he's run a race.

                         MAN/ACTOR
                    Wow! That went great. I think it
                    went great!

The man/actor hurries out the door.

17   INT. NICOLE, THE AGENT - AUDITION ROOM - CONTINUOUS

In the room, two people sit slightly apart at a table:
NICOLE, THE AGENT, a no-nonsense middle-aged woman, and EARL,
A PRODUCER, tanned and groomed in an expensive suit, the
collar open showing a gold chain. Behind and between them is
the CAMERA OPERATOR who films the auditions, the camera
mounted on a tripod. At another table, to the side of Nicole,
is Nicole's assistant, PAUL, a younger man, well-groomed and
sharp-dressed with a light sweater over his shoulders, the
sleeves tied loosely hanging on his chest. To the other side,
on a chair, is SANTIAGO, THE DIRECTOR, moody, intense. In a
chair next to him sits AMADO, AN INVESTOR, quiet, serious, a
money man. Both are Hispanic.

                         SANTIAGO
                    This is a waste of time. No one
                    we've seen is who I am looking for.

> NICOLE, THE AGENT
> There's one left. He wasn't
> originally scheduled but the
> picture on his resume looks
> interesting.

18   INT. NICOLE, THE AGENT - RECEPTION AREA - CONTINUOUS

> SALLY/RECEPTIONIST
> (her phone buzzes)
> You can go in now, Mr. Montana.

19   INT. NICOLE, THE AGENT - AUDITION ROOM - CONTINUOUS

The door opens and Montana enters.

> MONTANA
> Hello! Thank you for taking the
> time to see me. My name's Montana.

> NICOLE, THE AGENT
> Mr. Montana, hello. Please step
> forward and stand on the tape.

Montana sees on the floor a taped cross, marking the spot. He
positions himself over it.

> NICOLE, THE AGENT (CONT'D)
> According to your resume, your
> experience is rather limited. I see
> you played Hamlet. In a high school
> play?

> MONTANA
> 'Tis true! 'Tis true! Ah, there's
> the rub!

> NICOLE, THE AGENT
> And you've performed as a rodeo,
> *barrelman*. What is that?

> MONTANA
> They used to call them rodeo
> clowns. I'm a rodeo'er. A bull
> rider.
> (shows his belt buckle)
> Before and after my rides, I'd play
> the clown. You know, entertain the
> crowd, and divert the bull to keep
> the other bull riders safe.

                    NICOLE, THE AGENT
Hmm, I see. You are aware that the
film you're auditioning for is a
period piece, set in England,
during the time of Queen Elizabeth
I, the era of Shakespeare's most
prolific writings.

                    MONTANA
You bet! I saw that on the sides I
practiced while waiting. I think
I'm a perfect fit, especially with
my experience as Hamlet.

                    NICOLE, THE AGENT
Well, you do have the handsome,
movie star look.

                    MONTANA
          (suddenly shy, exaggerated
           drawl)
Aw shucks, now you're trying to
butter me up!
          (back to normal, tells
           them)
That's my Andy of Mayberry
imitation.
          (playing the part,
           grinding his toe on the
           floor)
You make me blush, trying to butter
me up like a biscuit!

                    PAUL, NICOLE'S ASSISTANT
          (eyes wide, licks his
           lips, sotto voce)
I'll butter you up like a biscuit!

                    NICOLE, THE AGENT
Okay. Please, give us your
monologue.

Montana visibly collects himself. Goes "into character":

                    MONTANA
Dung! The dung! The horror of the
dung. The cowards defile the name
of the king, with their cowardly
dung breath. I am sickened when I
look upon the dung eaters. Isis,
good Isis, I beseech thee...

                    NICOLE, THE AGENT
          (interrupting)
Okay! That's good! Montana, let me
be honest. It's the, uh, it's the
accent. I'm not sure it fits. Maybe
this isn't the right role for you.
But, thank you. We'll be in touch,
if we need you to come back.

                    MONTANA
Well, now, I'm sure you know, but
there was lot's of different kinds
of folks lived in London during
that time. There was accents from
all over. But if you want, I can do
the British accent.
          (collects himself, juts
           his chin)
I say, old chap, I will check my
shed-jule for the oh'klock of the
maffmatic too-tarr's arry-ivall.

                    NICOLE, THE AGENT
Okay! That's great! When we decide
to redo Deliverance on the River
Thames, you're the man!

                    MONTANA
          (surprised)
How'd you know I play the banjo?
Oh, that's right. It's on my
resume.

                    NICOLE, THE AGENT
I was thinking more in the line of
the two mountain men.

                    MONTANA
          (suddenly wary)
Wait a minute. Ya'll not doing
those gay porn flicks here, are ya?

                    NICOLE, THE AGENT
What?

                    MONTANA
Say, you know, back home I knew a
gal named Nicole. She was a fine
looking little filly. Man, what a
bod! She liked sex. Yep! She'd do
it anywhere, anytime.
          (MORE)

                    MONTANA (CONT'D)
          The only problem was, she had a
          medical condition, sometimes. The
          doctor called it a vaginal
          discharge.

Nicole, the Agent, her jaw drops open in shock. Earl, the
Producer, who'd sat stoically during the preceding action now
shows a look of animation on his face: SUDDEN SURPRISED
AMUSEMENT.

                    MONTANA (CONT'D)
          Yep. And when that happened, the
          discharge had an odor to it...

Nicole, Paul, Santiago, Amado, the Camera Operator, are all
staring at Montana with varying looks of shock and disbelief
on their faces. Only Earl is laughing.

                    NICOLE, THE AGENT
          Oh, my god!

                    EARL, A PRODUCER
               (smiling, stands, extends
                his arm for a handshake)
          Mr. Montana! Wow, it's been a rare
          pleasure to meet you.
               (guides Montana to the
                door)
          That was great. Thanks for coming
          by. We'll be in touch.

                    MONTANA
          I didn't catch your name.

                    EARL, A PRODUCER
          I'm Earl. The producer

                    MONTANA
          Good to meet you, Earl.

Montana exits through the door.

                    EARL, A PRODUCER
               (still amused, turns back
                to the others)
          You believe that? Let's take a
          break. Fifteen minutes.

Earl exits through the door.

20   EXT. HOLLYWOOD BOULEVARD - MOMENTS LATER

Earl comes out of the door of the building onto the sidewalk.
Earl looks both ways up and down the street. Earl see Montana
at his truck.

                    EARL, A PRODUCER
               (yells)
          Montana! Wait a minute.

Montana looks and sees Earl walking toward him. Montana goes
back to the sidewalk. They meet.

                    MONTANA
          Hey, Earl.

                    EARL, A PRODUCER
          Montana, have you done any stand-
          up? Any live comedy routines?

                    MONTANA
          Well, sure. We're always cutting up
          at the bar after the rodeo. Telling
          tall tales and such.

                    EARL, A PRODUCER
          I mean on stage, in front of an
          audience? Being filmed?

                    MONTANA
          Well, I just did. You guys were the
          audience, and there was the camera.
          I figured it was for real.

                    EARL, A PRODUCER
          I've got an interest in a bar, here
          in Hollywood, on Franklin Avenue.
          The name is Guerrilla Theatre. We
          have comedians do stand up. It's
          between North Bronson and Tamarind.
          Do you know the area?

                    MONTANA
          I can find it. What do you have in
          mind?

                    EARL, A PRODUCER
          We have open mic tonight. How'd you
          like to do a routine, on stage?
          What do you think?

                    MONTANA
          Sure! Wow, that'd be great. What
          time?

                    EARL, A PRODUCER
          Can you make it at nine PM? I'll be
          looking for you.

21   INT. HOLLYWOOD BOULEVARD - RESTAURANT - LATER

Montana is sitting at the counter, talking to Shirley.

                    SHIRLEY/WAITRESS
          There's ten thousand comedians in
          LA. About nine-thousand-nine-
          hundred and ninety of them are
          waiting tables in restaurants.

                    MONTANA
          Well, sure, I figure it's a long
          shot. But what the heck. Win, lose,
          or draw, it'll be fun. A blast. You
          couldn't pay me to miss it.

                    SHIRLEY/WAITRESS
          You've got the right attitude,
          Montana. Sure. Go for it. What the
          heck.

                    MONTANA
          Why don't you come by? Earl told me
          to be there at nine. I'm not sure
          when it'll be my turn, but I'll buy
          you a drink while we wait. How
          about it, Shirley?

                    SHIRLEY/WAITRESS
          Sure, Montana. Okay, I'll be there.

22   INT. MONTANA'S TRUCK - THE CAMPER - NIGHT

The camper has a bed area extending out over the truck roof,
inside the lower portion is a small u-shape table on one side
and a small propane stove the other side, its a typical
setup. Montana is standing by the table, searching in a
cardboard box.

                    MONTANA
                (mumbling to himself)
          There ya are! You rascal.

Montana sits a small box on the tabletop alongside another
larger box and some clothes on hangars. He begins to take off
the shirt he's wearing, to change into the other clothes.

23   EXT. FRANKLIN AV. - STREET PARKING - NIGHT

The rear door of the truck camper opens. In the light of a
streetlamp are seen FROM THE KNEE DOWN two legs. A FOOT steps
out onto the metal stair tread. The leg is inside a pair of
blue jeans with a sharp cowboy-tux-style ironed and starched
crease, and the foot is inside a top-quality leather cowboy
boot with stainless steel spurs.

24   EXT. GUERRILLA THEATRE - FRONT DOOR - NIGHT

MONTANA'S P.O.V.: as he walks to and opens the door and
enters.

25   INT. GUERRILLA THEATRE - CONTINUOUS

MONTANA'S P.O.V. cont.: As he is WALKING through the
vestibule, into the lounge, Montana SEES a raised stage on
his left, and SEES the bar on the right. Between are tables
and chairs full of customers who are laughing, talking,
drinking, waiting for the show to begin.

26   INT. GUERRILLA THEATRE - AT THE BAR - CONTINUOUS

MONTANA'S P.O.V. cont.: SEES Earl, leaning on the end of the
bar.

                    MONTANA
          Hey, Earl. How ya doin?

                    EARL, A PRODUCER
          Hi, Montana. Our first act didn't
          show. You ready to go? Wanna bust
          your cheery?

27   INT. GUERRILLA THEATRE - THE STAGE, LEFT WING- MOMENTS LATER

MONTANA'S P.O.V. cont.: Earl is on the stage, standing at the
microphone.

                    EARL, A PRODUCER
          Ladies and gentlemen. It gives me
          great pleasure to introduce you to
          Montana. Montana just arrived in
          town this morning and this is his
          debut on stage. A big welcome - for
          Montana!

28   INT. GUERRILLA THEATRE - THE STAGE - CONTINUOUS

MONTANA'S P.O.V. cont.: WALKS to downstage center, to the microphone on a stand. He SEES the crowd looking at him, watching, waiting, expectant.

CAMERA'S P.O.V.: Now CLOSE ON Montana, his face under the brim of the hat.

                    MONTANA
          Howdy, folks. Wow, this is
          fantastic! Earl, thanks for the
          invite.

29   INT. GUERRILLA THEATRE - AT THE BAR - CONTINUOUS

Shirley is sitting at the bar, a drink in hand. For the FIRST TIME WE SEE Montana STRAIGHT ON from **SHIRLEY'S P.O.V.** Montana is dressed in a high-end, top-dollar, western outfit. He looks like an ambassador for the rodeo, or a country-western star-singer. From the Stetson on his head to the exotic skin boots, the sharp jeans, the embroidered tan western-cut leather sport coat, the black cowboy snap-button shirt, the bolo around his neck with matching belt buckle, all the way down to a set of shiny stainless steel spurs. The outfit looks natural on Montana, a perfect fit. In Montana's hand he holds a banjo by the top of the neck.

At the bar next to Shirley are THREE PRETTY YOUNG LADIES, dressed up and ready to party.

                    1ST LADY AT BAR
          Well, howdy-doodie, cowboy!

                    2ND LADY AT BAR
          I'll go to the rodeo with him!

                    3RD LADY AT BAR
          Ride me, cowboy!

Shirley, hearing their comments, smiles and nods her head.

                    SHIRLEY/WAITRESS
                  (sotto voce)
          Alright, Montana, you're on.

30   INT. GUERRILLA THEATRE - THE STAGE - CONTINUOUS

Montana lifts the banjo, his fingers cut a quick chord. He looks comfortable and at ease.

                    MONTANA
You might not know it, from looking
at me, that I'm a rodeo cowboy.
Yep, anyway, I was, until a couple
months ago, when a bull busted my
hip in Montana.
          (banjo & singing)
I'm a rodeo cowboy, I've seen the
sights, But now I'm in the city
under neon lights. The concrete
jungle, it ain't quite the same, As
ridin' them bulls, in a rodeo game!
          (end singing)
I thought I'd come to Hollywood and
try out a new occupation. So I sure
appreciate your warm welcome. I've
been rodeo'in about five years.
Loved every minute of it. Hated to
give it up. The doc said I had to.
So, I'm aiming to find a career in
film and on stage. Now I have to
warn you, that I don't know how to
be - how do they say it? - oh yeah,
"Politically Correct." Where I come
from and on the roads I've traveled
since then, everybody and
everything is fair game. So, let me
tell you about the rodeo, and how
it, like everything else in this
crazy world is changing.

Montana blends the banjo into his routine.

                MONTANA (CONT'D)
          (banjo & singing)
In this crazy changin' world, we're
caught in a whirl, Where time keeps
spinnin' faster, like a wild-eyed
squirrel.
          (end singing)
About a year ago I went to compete
in a rodeo, it was in a town in
northwest Texas, near the Oklahoma
line, right smack dab in the middle
of cowboy country. I'd not heard of
this rodeo before, but the prize
money was top dollar. I was close
anyway, so I mailed in my fee, then
a few days later took off driving
from Tucson.
                    (MORE)

MONTANA (CONT'D)

Now, I didn't study the details
about this particular rodeo too
close, which was all my fault, so
you can imagine my surprise when I
got there to find out it was a Gay
drag queen rodeo!
          (banjo & singing)
*There's an ugly girl with a heart
of gold, In a world that judges by
what they're told. But her beauty
shines from deep within, With a
good soul, she'll always win.*
          (end singing)
This drag queen stuff has been all
over the news lately. Some folks
are pretty fired up about it, some
for and some against. And I know
it's a sensitive subject to some
people, one way or the other. Now I
have to tell you, I believe that
the human condition, as the
philosophers call it, is tough. As
the farmer says, it's a hard row to
hoe. And I believe that the only
way to deal with the absurdity of
it all is to find the humor in it.
So I'm going to tell you what
happened to me at that rodeo. It
was a good joke on me, I admit it,
but I can laugh about it and at
myself. I hope you can see the
humor in it too. So, here we go.
It was a sunup to sundown drive.
Seven hundred miles of not much to
see except dry brown land in every
direction. I finally get there,
climb my sore old ass out of the
truck, and take a first good look
around. Well, I darn near busted a
gut laughing. I'm standing there
gasping and choking. I can't
breathe I'm laughing so hard.
          (banjo & singing)
*They may laugh and they may tease,
But she holds her head up with such
ease. For she knows that looks can
deceive, It's the goodness inside
that we should believe.*
          (end singing)
I must have looked like I was
having a fit or convulsions or
something. These two fellows were
walking by - holding hands!
          (MORE)

MONTANA (CONT'D)
They were all gussied up in
transvestite outfits. The tall
skinny one was wearing a white
wedding gown dress, he, she, says
to me, "Are you alright?" Well, I
couldn't help myself, I had to ask,
"Where do you guys go shopping?"
And I laughed. I reckon they
figured I was making fun of them,
because they get all offended, like
I insulted them. The tall skinny
one tells me, "Maybe you should get
on back to redneck-ville where you
came from. Shithead!" The other
one, his, her, husband, was this
short muscular dude with several
days of whiskers on his face and a
black eye from a bar fight. He was
all pretty'ed up with lipstick and
rouge and whatnot. He had a blonde
wig sticking out from under his
pink cowboy hat. He was wearing
pink cowboy boots. He was dressed
in a little pink ballerina tutu
with his white hairy legs showing.
He had on a pink bra with falsies,
showing these big fake pointy
titties under an unbuttoned sheer
pink blouse. The bra was mashing
down this mess of black monkey-
looking hair on his chest. He was a
sight, I kid you not!
        (banjo & singing)
*Oh, don't you see, beauty's more
than skin, In her heart, there's a
light that's shining within. In
this world so cruel, she's a beacon
of grace, That ugly girl with a
beautiful soul's embrace.*
        (end singing)
The short guy gets a surly look on
his face, then tells me in this
deep baritone voice, he says, "I'll
squash you like a bug, boy!" Then
he looks at his tall skinny husband
and says with a girlish giggle in a
high-pitched voice, "He is kinda
cute, though, isn't he." I was
horrified. You've never seen such a
bunch of ugly looking wanna-be
women in your life!
        (banjo & singing)
            (MORE)

                    MONTANA (CONT'D)
          So let's celebrate this girl so
          kind, For her beauty's rare, a
          precious find. In a world that's
          often quick to judge, It's her
          inner beauty we should never
          begrudge.
                    (end singing)
          I jumped in my truck and hauled ass
          out of there! I was smoking the
          tires! I didn't know my truck could
          go that fast. I still have
          nightmares about it. And I never
          did get that entry fee refunded!
                    (banjo & singing)
          Yes, she's the one with a heart so
          pure, Her love and kindness will
          always endure. In this banjo's
          tune, her story we've told, Of two
          ugly girls with hearts of gold.
                    (end singing)

The crowd has set silent during Montana's monologue.

31   INT. GUERRILLA THEATRE - THE BAR - CONTINUOUS

Shirley's P.O.V.: as she studies the crowd, watching for
their reaction. A long moment passes.

32   INT. GUERRILLA THEATRE - AT A TABLE - MOMENTS LATER

FOUR WOMEN suddenly bust out laughing. THEIR VOICES are DEEP
and MANLY. These four women are actually FOUR MEN IN DRAG.
They are dressed in evening gowns and wigs and etcetera, they
look ready for the model's catwalk. They begin howling
laughing, beating the table with their fists. Their hilarity
is infectious, and the rest of the audience busts up
laughing.

                                        DISSOLVE TO:

33   INT. GUERRILLA THEATRE - THE STAGE - LATER

ANOTHER COMEDIAN is finishing up his act.

                    ANOTHER COMEDIAN
                    (struggling)
          Th-Th-Th...That's all, folks!

The crowd applauds politely.

34   INT. GUERRILLA THEATRE - THE BAR - CONTINUOUS

Montana is leaning on the bar, talking to Shirley.

                    SHIRLEY/WAITRESS
          Your skit was funny. It was good.
          You caught the audience off guard.

                    MONTANA
          Ahh, that was kind of lame really.
          I didn't want to scare them off.
          I've got some that are pretty
          raunchy. It's hard to get rodeo'ers
          to laugh but I've managed, here and
          there.

Earl has walked up while Montana was talking.

                    EARL, A PRODUCER
          You got more? How'd you like to do
          an encore?

                    MONTANA
          Well, sure! The more the merrier.

35   INT. GUERRILLA THEATRE - THE STAGE - MOMENTS LATER

                    MONTANA
          Before I came here tonight, I
          stopped for dinner at a restaurant
          in Beverly Hills. It was one of
          those places where you might see a
          movie star. I didn't see any movie
          stars but the place was full of
          tourists who were paying about a
          hundred bucks for a cheeseburger,
          hoping they'd see a movie star.
          It's a pretty good scam. I wish I'd
          thought of it.
               (banjo & singing)
          *Well, I'm a-tellin' you a tale
          'bout folks so keen, Tourists in
          Beverly Hills, a sight to be seen.*
               (end singing)
          Anyway, they design these
          restaurants now with all these hard
          surfaces and open floor plans that
          make them loud, so the space is
          like one big echo chamber. It's
          hard to hear people because of the
          noise, so everybody has to shout.
                    (MORE)

MONTANA (CONT'D)
There were four ladies sitting at
the table next to mine, they were
all talking loud. I didn't mean to
eavesdrop but unless I plugged my
ears I couldn't help but hear what
they were saying. One lady said,
"So, tell us about your date with
the new guy. What happened? How was
it?"...

CUT TO:

36   EXT. TRAFFIC ON SURFACE STREET - NIGHT

LAPD SWAT. THREE COMMERCIAL HEAVY-DUTY TRUCKS, painted in
official black with white letters, are moving fast. FOCUS ON
the lead truck which is the MOBILE COMMAND POST (MCP) that
has a large enclosed cargo space at the rear.

37   I/E. MOBILE COMMAND POST - CONTINUOUS

In TACTICAL ASSAULT UNIFORMS are A DRIVER and a NAVIGATOR in
front. Seen through an opening between the seats, in the rear
cargo space, sitting at built-in work stations, is the SWAT
OFFICER IN CHARGE, and a TECHNOLOGY SPECIALIST who works the
AUDIO/VIDEO EQUIPMENT.

SWAT OFFICER IN CHARGE
(talking into headset mic)
Ten minutes.

38   EXT. TRAFFIC ON SURFACE STREET - CONTINUOUS

FOCUS on the second truck which is the SWAT ARMORED PERSONNEL
CARRIER (APC) designed like the first truck. A SHOT from
OUTSIDE the windshield looking in shows a DRIVER TWO and
NAVIGATOR TWO. Seen through an opening between the seats is
the rear cargo space.

39   I/E. SWAT ARMORED PERSONNEL CARRIER - CONTINUOUS

In the back of the APC, sitting on benches each side of the
truck, are SWAT TEAM MEMBERS in ASSAULT UNIFORMS, each has a
rifle in hand. At the front end of the starboard side bench
is the TACTICAL TEAM OPERATOR.

TACTICAL TEAM OPERATOR
(into microphone)
Roger that. Ten minutes.
(MORE)

                    TACTICAL TEAM OPERATOR (CONT'D)
                 (to team members)
          Ten minutes. Saddle up.

The TWO TEAM MEMBERS sitting at the rear on each side stand
and hook their belt harnesses onto the truck walls. Then they
raise the garage door at the rear of the truck, showing the
outside. Behind them is the THIRD TRUCK that's pulling a
TRAILER with a piece of HEAVY EQUIPMENT loaded on it.

40   EXT. TRAFFIC ON SURFACE STREET - CONTINUOUS

A quick PAN around the third truck shows this is a CREW CAB
FLATBED with tool boxes on the back.The truck has four doors
and is carrying FIVE MEN INSIDE, the DRIVER THREE and
NAVIGATOR THREE in the front and three TEAM MEMBERS in the
rear seat. The truck pulls a trailer that is loaded with an
ARMORED ASSAULT VEHICLE (AAV). The AAV has a long sturdy
metal BATTERING RAM attached to the front.

41   I/E. CREW CAB FLATBED - CONTINUOUS

                       NAVIGATOR THREE
                 (hand at earphone,
                  listening)
          Ten minutes.

                                                   CUT TO:

42   INT. GUERRILLA THEATRE - THE STAGE - CONTINUOUS

                          MONTANA
          The other lady says, "It was a
          typical first date. He took me to
          dinner and a movie. It was a PG
          movie, you know, a family thing." I
          hear another lady say, "Well? What
          happened?" Then, "We got our
          popcorn and sat down. The movie
          started, and pretty soon there was
          a scene with a man and a woman. I
          forget what they were talking
          about, but they weren't doing
          anything, you know, sexual. The man
          leaned close and gave the woman a
          friendly kiss on the cheek. The guy
          I'm with, my new date, he yells out
          - FUCK HER, BUDDY!
                          (MORE)

MONTANA (CONT'D)
I was horrified but all the other
people in the audience busted out
laughing." The other three women
crack up, saying "OMG!" and "Are
you serious?" and then the three
ladies ask her, "Then what
happened?"

CUT TO:

43   EXT. TRAFFIC ON SURFACE STREET - NIGHT

The three LAPD SWAT trucks stop at an intersection in a
residential area. The doors open and the Team Members move
efficiently out to their assigned positions and duties at the
TARGET RESIDENCE.

44   EXT. TARGET RESIDENCE - CONTINUOUS

1) The five men in the truck that was pulling the trailer
prepare the ARMORED ASSAULT VEHICLE (AAV). One man enters the
cab of the AAV;

2) two of the men lower the rear ramp of the trailer;

3) the man in the cab, the OPERATOR, straps his safety belt
on and pushes the start button;

4) the AAV, rolling on rubber tank treads, exits the trailer,
then pulls around facing the direction of the trucks;

5) eight Team Members, SNIPER-COUNTER-SNIPERS, carrying
RIFLES with TELESCOPIC SIGHTS, deploy to their positions;

6) one pair goes to the brick pillars of the entry gate at
the street end of the driveway;

7) another pair climb over the neighbors wall and hunker down
by the swimming pool in the rear;

8) the other two pairs go to the left and right sides of the
TARGET RESIDENCE;

45   I/E. MOBILE COMMAND POST - CONTINUOUS

The truck interior lights are dimmed. MULTIPLE MONITORS show
the action from a POLE MOUNTED CAMERA ON THE TRUCK ROOF and
BODY CAM footage from Team Members.

OFFICER IN CHARGE
(viewing a screen, says
into microphone)
The street light is backlighting
sniper team one. Take out the front
street light.

46   EXT. TARGET RESIDENCE - CONTINUOUS

Out on the street a Team Member with a SILENT HI-TECH AIR
RIFLE shoots the street light. The street area is plunged
into darkness.

                                                    CUT TO:

47   INT. GUERRILLA THEATRE - THE STAGE - CONTINUOUS

                    MONTANA
          She says, "About twenty minutes
          later, he does it again! A
          different man and woman were
          together on the screen, the man
          reached out and took hold of he
          woman's hand, and he yelled - FUCK
          HER, BUDDY!" The other three women
          are laughing, one says, "Then what
          happened?"...

                                                    CUT TO:

48   EXT. TARGET RESIDENCE - NIGHT - CONTINUOUS

The AAV is now in the street facing the Target Residence, it
rolls up over the curb and races across the grass toward the
front of the Target Residence:

1) On the left and right sides of front door the Team Members
are lined up, prepared for entry;

2) another group of Team Members are in close formation,
running behind the AAV as it makes the approach;

3) the BATTERING RAM at the front of the AAV smashes into the
FRONT DOOR of the Target Residence, BANG, knocking the door
down, making a forced entry;

4) the AAV reverses and the Team Members approach the entry,
the two men in front at each side toss FLASH BANG GRENADES
into the breached front door of the Target Residence. Then
the Team expertly infiltrates into the Target Residence.

TACTICAL TEAM OPERATOR
(through a loudspeaker)
POLICE. SHOW YOUR HANDS. POLICE.
SHOW YOUR HANDS.

CUT TO:

49   INT. GUERRILLA THEATRE - THE STAGE - CONTINUOUS

MONTANA
The lady tells her friends, "I was
so embarrassed. I was hiding down
in my seat! Some of the audience
laughed, but not all, because it
was a sad scene. The little girl's
puppy got ran over by a car!" The
other ladies go, "Oh. That's
terrible! What did he do then?" And
the lady says, "He was sitting
there giggling!" A lady asks her,
"He was giggling about the dead
puppy doggie?" She says, "No, I
think he was giggling because he
thought he was being so funny!"

CUT TO:

50   INT. TARGET RESIDENCE - NIGHT - CONTINUOUS

The Team Members expertly go room to room in the residence,
storming in.

TEAM MEMBER
POLICE. POLICE. SHOW YOUR HANDS.

51   INT. TARGET RESIDENCE - BEDROOM - CONTINUOUS

The sudden light from high intensity flashlights reveal the
previously seen first man and one of the previously seen
women sitting straight up on the bed, apparently jerked from
sleep. The woman screams and covers her head with the
blanket. The man leaps from the bed and tries to run. He is
tackled and subdued.

CUT TO:

52   INT. GUERRILLA THEATRE - THE STAGE - CONTINUOUS

                         MONTANA
              The lady tells her friends, "He did
              it again, right at the end of the
              movie, at the funeral. When the
              dead man's friend gave the widow a
              comforting hug and a little kiss on
              her cheek. He yelled - FUCK HER,
              BUDDY! I thought I'd die!" A lady
              asked her, "So then what happened?"
              She says, "Well, we walked down the
              street, to a club, and had a
              drink." A lady asks her, "And then
              what happened?" She says, "Then we
              went to his place." A lady asks,
              "Well, did he, you know - fuck her,
              buddy?" The lady says, in kind of a
              surprised voice, "Uh, duh. Well,
              yeah!" The other three are
              laughing, I hear them clinking
              glasses, saying "Cheers!" Then one
              asked her, "Are you going to see
              him again?" And the lady says,
              "Well, yeah!"
                   (banjo & singing)
              She fell for a man with a humor
              absurd and offensive, His jokes
              were so twisted, she couldn't
              resisted.
                   (end singing)

         His left hand holding the neck, Montana raises his banjo to
         the air in salute.

                         MONTANA (CONT'D)
              Thank ya, folks. You're great. Just
              remember, no matter where ya go,
              there ya are!

                                                       CUT TO:

53   INT. TARGET RESIDENCE - NIGHT - LATER

         FEDERAL AGENTS and LAPD SWAT have the raided house under
         control. The residents are handcuffed, lying on the floor
         like landed fish. The FEDS are searching the rooms of the
         house. Opening the door of a room with a curtained window
         they see CASH COUNTING MACHINES and BANKERS BOXES and GUNS.

         An AGENT removes the lid of a bankers box to see CASH STACKED
         in neat bundles.

                        AGENT
                  Bingo!

54   EXT. OVERHEAD VIEW - DOWNTOWN LOS ANGELES, CA - MORNING

        ZOOM on a building that houses GOVERNMENT OFFICES.

55   INT. UNITED STATES ATTORNEY'S OFFICE FOR THE CENTRAL DISTRICT
        OF CALIFORNIA - PRESS BRIEFING ROOM - CONTINUOUS

        Journalists, photographers and video crews are listening to a
        DOJ SPOKESPERSON who is standing at a podium with the
        Department of Justice shield displayed.

                        DOJ SPOKESPERSON
                  The United States Department of the
                  Treasury's Office of Foreign Assets
                  Control announces a major law
                  enforcement action under the
                  Foreign Narcotics Kingpin
                  Designation Act. Last night's raid
                  was a continuation of Project
                  Python.

56   INT. UPSCALE HOME - LIVING ROOM - CONTINUOUS

        Through the windows is a view of a custom swimming pool and
        patio in a landscaped backyard. Amado, the Investor, and
        Santiago, the Director are watching the DOJ Press Briefing on
        a big screen TV.

57   INT. UNITED STATES ATTORNEY'S OFFICE FOR THE CENTRAL DISTRICT
        OF CALIFORNIA - PRESS BRIEFING ROOM - CONTINUOUS

                        DOJ SPOKESPERSON
                  This operation was conducted by
                  Homeland Security Investigations,
                  the Drug Enforcement
                  Administration, the Federal Bureau
                  of Investigation, and the Los
                  Angeles Police Department.

                        REPORTER
                  What was the reason for the raid?

                        DOJ SPOKESPERSON
                  The Sinaloa Cartel is responsible
                  for over 90% of all illicit drug
                  smuggling into the United States.

                    ANOTHER REPORTER
          This was a drug bust? How much
          drugs were recovered?

                    DOJ SPOKESPERSON
          The cartel smuggles heroin,
          fentanyl, methamphetamines, and
          cocaine. Fentanyl was responsible
          for over 70,000 overdoses last year
          in the United States. But this was
          not just a drug raid, it was a
          strike at the very heart of the
          Cartel's money laundering
          operation.

58   INT. UPSCALE HOME - LIVING ROOM - CONTINUOUS

       Amado, and Santiago, continue watching the press briefing.

59   INT. UNITED STATES ATTORNEY'S OFFICE FOR THE CENTRAL DISTRICT
       OF CALIFORNIA - PRESS BRIEFING ROOM - CONTINUOUS

                    DOJ SPOKESPERSON
          To evade sanctions and gain access
          to the financial system the cartel
          uses legitimate American businesses
          to launder their drug proceeds. The
          cartel is investing in real estate
          companies, industrial and
          agricultural companies, boutique
          hotels, bars, nightclubs, and the
          entertainment industry. Everything
          from mom and pop stores in strip
          malls to Fortune 500 corporations.
          Certain banks are involved in the
          transfer and laundering of over
          thirty billion dollars per year in
          drug revenues.

                    A THIRD REPORTER
          What was found at the house that
          was raided in this operation last
          night?

60   INT. HOLLYWOOD BOULEVARD - RESTAURANT - CONTINUOUS

       Montana, sitting at the counter drinking a cup of coffee, and
       Shirley, and Bob, standing nearby, are watching the TV screen
       showing the DOJ press briefing.

61   INT. UNITED STATES ATTORNEY'S OFFICE FOR THE CENTRAL DISTRICT
OF CALIFORNIA - PRESS BRIEFING ROOM - CONTINUOUS

>DOJ SPOKESPERSON
>This particular target was a
>collection point, where cash was
>counted and stored. In this
>residence was seized seventeen
>million dollars in cash.

62   INT. UPSCALE HOME - LIVING ROOM - CONTINUOUS

Amado jerks to his feet with a curse:

>AMADO
>Jesucristo!

63   INT. HOLLYWOOD BOULEVARD - RESTAURANT - CONTINUOUS

>SHIRLEY/WAITRESS
>Seventeen million dollars! Cash!

>BOB/MANAGER
>Right down the street. Imagine
>that?

>MONTANA
>(whistles, impressed)
>Imagine that.

64   INT. UNITED STATES ATTORNEY'S OFFICE FOR THE CENTRAL DISTRICT
OF CALIFORNIA - PRESS BRIEFING ROOM - CONTINUOUS

>DOJ SPOKESPERSON
>Also confiscated was cocaine,
>heroin, fentanyl powder, two dozen
>unregistered firearms, and arrested
>were six suspects. This raid tells
>the cartel, you will not operate in
>Los Angeles, California.

65   INT. HOLLYWOOD BOULEVARD - RESTAURANT - MOMENTS LATER

The press briefing has ended. Bob uses the remote to lower
the volume. Montana begins reading aloud an article in the
daily newspaper. Shirley and Bob are listening.

                    MONTANA
This reporter, he writes, quote -
"since the invention of stage
performance, there hasn't been such
rude, filthy sounding trash heard
until this Montana shows up" -
unquote. I guess he won't want my
autograph.

                    BOB/MANAGER
You're famous, Montana. That's a
world record. First day. First gig.
A write-up in the next morning's
paper.

                    SHIRLEY/WAITRESS
I know that guy. He's a jerk. He's
not a staffer, he's a guest opinion
writer. It's lucky for you he was
in the audience last night. All
he's done is give you free
publicity. So, what's next,
Montana?

                    MONTANA
Earl wants me to come back Saturday
night. In the meantime, I'm going
to try and find an agent.

                    BOB/MANAGER
What you need is a business
manager. The agents will come to
you, if your manager gets you the
right attention.

                    MONTANA
Yeah? How does that work?

                    BOB/MANAGER
Your business manager is long term,
helping with planning your career.
An agent looks to get you booked
right now, so the money rolls in. I
got in the restaurant business part-
time, years ago, while I acted. I
had some extra gigs but, like most
actors, never got that big break. A
business manager can help you get
that break.

                    MONTANA
Can you recommend a business
manager?

                    BOB/MANAGER
          Shirley knows the business inside
          and out.

                    SHIRLEY/WAITRESS
          Me?

                    BOB/MANAGER
          Sure. Why not. Montana, you can
          count on Shirley being straight and
          honest with you. Which is more than
          can be said about most people in
          the industry. Give it a shot. I'll
          work your schedule around it.

                    MONTANA
          Sounds good to me, Shirley. What do
          you say?

66   EXT. GUERRILLA THEATRE - DAY

          Shirley walks to the front door.

67   INT. GUERRILLA THEATRE - THE OFFICE - MOMENTS LATER

          Earl is at his desk, looking at a PAPER DOCUMENT. Shirley
          sits in a seat next to the desk.

                    SHIRLEY/WAITRESS
          This town is cruel. It eats people
          like zombies. Montana's going to
          need some help getting situated.

                    EARL, A PRODUCER
          Montana's a natural. He's got the
          look, the material, the delivery,
          the timing. He can go far.

                    SHIRLEY/WAITRESS
          That's right. And I'm going to help
          him.

                    EARL, A PRODUCER
          This seems fair. Sure.
               (signs the document)

                    SHIRLEY/WAITRESS
          Montana has what he calls his
          "working philosophy."

                    EARL, A PRODUCER
          What's that?

                    SHIRLEY/WAITRESS
          Montana says, "You be fair to me.
          I'll be fair to you."

68   EXT. HOLLYWOOD - APARTMENT BUILDING - DAY

          Shirley and Montana are on the sidewalk, approaching the
          glass entrance doors.

                    SHIRLEY/WAITRESS
                I know the owner. This one bedroom
                has sat vacant for months now.
                Believe me, that's unusual for this
                neighborhood, especially since the
                rent has been lowered.

          Montana holds the front door open for Shirley, they enter.

69   INT. APARTMENT - MOMENTS LATER

          Shirley and Montana are standing inside the small but snug
          apartment. It's unfurnished, clean, ready for move in.

                    MONTANA
                How long did the body lay in here,
                before it was found?

                    SHIRLEY/WAITRESS
                Almost a week. The guy was sitting
                in a chair.
                    (points at a window and AC
                    unit)
                Right there, in front of the air
                conditioner. The AC was set on low.
                I guess the cold air helped to, you
                know, slow down the, uh, process.

                    MONTANA
                And how long ago was that?

                    SHIRLEY/WAITRESS
                It was at the end of the pandemic,
                the end of 2021.

                    MONTANA
                It's set empty for almost two
                years?

                    SHIRLEY/WAITRESS
                No. There's been four people move
                in and out. They wouldn't stay.
                They said it's haunted.

                    MONTANA
          Haunted? No joke? You mean like a
          real ghost? Wow! That's cool.

                SHIRLEY/WAITRESS
          Do you believe in ghosts, Montana?

                    MONTANA
          No, I don't. All that supernatural
          stuff is just people's imaginations
          running wild.

                SHIRLEY/WAITRESS
          You don't believe in ghosts,
          spirits, angels, any of that stuff?

                    MONTANA
          Maybe I don't have any imagination
          or whatever but, no, I don't. I've
          personally never seen anything like
          that or even felt a tickle of it.
          And I don't know anybody who has
          either. What about you, Shirley, do
          you believe in that stuff?

                SHIRLEY/WAITRESS
          Oh, I don't know. Maybe some days I
          do, some days I don't. It's a
          mystery.

                    MONTANA
          Yeah, I guess it's like religion.
          It's hard to prove one way or the
          other.

Montana suddenly looks over Shirley's shoulder and points.

                MONTANA (CONT'D)
               (sharply)
          What's that?

Shirley turns her head to look behind her.

                MONTANA (CONT'D)
          BOO!

Shirley jumps like she'd been poked with a stick. Quickly
turns back to Montana.

                SHIRLEY/WAITRESS
          Ha hah! Very funny! Ten thousand
          comedians out of a job and I get
          stuck with you!

Shirley gives Montana an exaggerated punch on his arm.
Montana "acts" the pain.

                    MONTANA
          Ow! That hurt!

                    SHIRLEY/WAITRESS
          Ha, hah. Rodeo clown! Alright,
          look, the apartment was stripped
          out and completely redone after the
          guy died. Then it was cleaned again
          after the other tenants left. You
          need to get out of that truck.
          Sleeping on the side of the road
          and using the gym shower, you're
          going to be too busy to hassle with
          all that. I'll handle the lease
          paperwork. And I'll call the
          furniture rental place to get you a
          bed, couch and stuff.

                    MONTANA
          Okay, Shirley. I like that it's
          handy to the Guerrilla Theatre,
          right around the corner.
               (looking out the window)
          Hey, you know the bonus is the view
          of that building across the street.
          That's some mansion. Who lives
          there?

Through the window is seen a tan, stone, six-story, French
chateau, located in lush landscaping behind black metal
security fencing.

                    SHIRLEY/WAITRESS
          Oh, that's some outer space alien
          UFO guy, named Xenu. He lives there
          with his crazy cult followers. Stay
          away from them. They'll try to sell
          you stuff.

70   I/E. CAR DRIVING ON THE 405 FREEWAY - EVENING

Two men are inside the car: Santiago is driving, Amado is in
the passenger seat. The car goes past a SIGN indicating the
car is approaching the exit for CENTURY BOULEVARD and the LAX
AIRPORT. The car turns onto the exit.

71   EXT. HOTEL - PARKING LOT - MOMENTS LATER

The car drives into the hotel parking lot. Amado and Santiago
exit the car and walk toward the front door of the hotel.

72   INT. HOTEL - GUEST ROOM - MOMENTS LATER

In the room are Amado and Santiago and another man, PABLO
PEREZ who is in his forties, he is casually dressed but in
expensive clothing, a gold watch on his wrist. Pablo Perez
sits in a chair, the window at his back, the curtains open.
Pablo's face is semi-shaded while the sunlight shines on
Santiago and Amado, standing before him, being questioned.

(SUBTITLES IN ENGLISH)

                    PABLO PEREZ
            El jefe quiere saber cómo sucedió
            esto. (The boss wants to know how
            this happened.)

                    AMADO
            Pablo. No sé. Tal vez la policía
            tuvo suerte. (Pablo. I don't know.
            Maybe the police got lucky.)

                    PABLO PEREZ
                (jerks a thumb over his
                shoulder, indicating a
                direction)
            El gran jefe no cree en la suerte.
            (The big boss does not believe in
            luck.)

Pablo turns his head to look behind and to the side of them.
FOCUS ON Earl who is standing at the open interconnecting
door from the adjoining room.

                    EARL, A PRODUCER
            Yo tampoco creo en la suerte. (I
            don't believe in luck either.)

                    PABLO PEREZ
            Entonces, ¿quién es la rata? (So,
            who is the rat?)

73   INT. GUERRILLA THEATRE - THE STAGE - NIGHT

A different show as evidenced by Montana's change of attire
and the different crowd, Montana is at the microphone.

MONTANA

I'm one of those people who never
had children. I'm a confirmed
bachelor. I like being a bachelor.
One time I did get married, to a
crazy redhead woman, but I only
made that mistake because I had a
brain injury. No kidding. I got
thrown by a bull and landed on my
head. That wasn't unusual and I'd
have walked away from it except the
bull turned around and kicked me
right on the temple. I was in a
coma for about a month, and when I
woke up, well, my brains were
scrambled up and I wasn't thinking
real straight, so I got married.
    (banjo & singing)
Well, there once was a cowboy, a
bit dim in the head, Took a kick
from a bull, left his brains all
scattered and spread. He met a wild
redhead, crazy as can be, Said,
"Darlin', let's get hitched," and
she hollered, "Yippee!"
    (end singing)
Long story short, that union lasted
about five years, then we got
divorced. Like I said, I never had
kids, so I don't have a lot of
information about raising them.
Except that all the people I've met
who do have kids tell me the same
thing. They say, "I love my kids,
but if I had to do it over
again..." They mostly don't finish
that sentence but it's the thought
that counts, right? One guy I know,
a hardworking man who does manual
labor all day, he told me, in a
real tired voice, "If I hadn't had
these kids, I'd gone down a
different hole." When he said that
he looked and sounded so depressed
it made me depressed! I had to go
to happy hour at the bar to get
better again.
    (banjo & singing)
He's a sad cowboy in a happy hour
town, Lookin' for a smile as the
sun's goin' down. With a whiskey in
his hand, and a tear in his eye,
He's hopin' that this honky-tonk
will teach him how to fly.
            (MORE)

MONTANA (CONT'D)
(end singing)
There's one thing about raising
kids that, just the thought of it,
horrifies me. That's pottie
training! Who in their right mind
would sign up for such a job? I've
done some research on the subject,
and according to the experts on the
Internet, the first year alone a
baby will need 3,000 diaper
changes! It can take three years
for a child to be pottie trained
and can take about 8,000 diaper
changes! 8,000 dirty diapers! The
horror! The horror!
(banjo & singing)
*Well, there's a smell in the air,
and it ain't no rose, Daddy's
holdin' up that diaper, and holdin'
his nose! He's lookin' at the mess,
sayin', "What have we here?" It's a
dirty ol' diaper, and he's full of
fear!*
(end singing)
How do parents do it? How do you
train the little bastards to go on
the kiddie pottie seat? One guy I
know told me that, like a coach,
you have to talk them through the
process. Daddy tells the kid,
"Look. Make a face like this
(*Montana makes an ugly face*) now
grunt, and push" -- like the little
bastard is in labor, giving birth
to an alien, like in the movie, but
instead of popping out the chest it
pops out the back there! "Push!
Push" splash, yippee! It finally
worked! Daddy is so happy! Daddy
says, "It's a miracle! No more of
those stinking diapers!"
(banjo & singing)
*Now, he's almost through, and he's
startin' to grin, He's conquered
that diaper, and he's in it to win.
So, here's to all the daddies,
who've faced the dirty test,
Changed a million diapers, and
still gave it their best. Though it
may be messy, and it sure ain't
fun, They'll do it all with love,
for their precious little one!*
(end singing)
And then, what happens? Uh, oh.
(MORE)

                    MONTANA (CONT'D)
It's family night at the
restaurant, or the movies, or god
forbid, at Sunday morning church,
and the little bastard has an
accident - with no diaper on,
because daddy thought the little
bastard was all trained. Daddy's
stomping around, raising hell. "The
dog got trained better than that!
Is our kid some kind of idiot?" The
kid's all crying and shit. This is
a traumatic experience! Now mommy
has to calm daddy down, and at the
same time tell the kid, "No honey,
you're not an idiot. Daddy's just a
little upset. You'll do better next
time, right?" Kids! Pottie
training! The whole things like a
nightmare! Like a horror movie!
          (banjo & singing)
In the depths of a diaper, a
monster did dwell, A horror movie
tale, you won't dare to tell. With
a stinky surprise, it would leap
and attack, Leaving trails of
chaos, leaving parents in shock.
          (end singing)
Why would anyone volunteer for such
a job? And the craziest thing is,
daddies and mommies don't learn
from their first mistake. They keep
making more babies! Haven't they
figured out what causes that?
Goodnight, folks. Just remember, no
matter where ya go, there ya are!

                              DISSOLVE TO:

74   INT. MONTANA'S APARTMENT - DAY

Montana and Shirley are sitting at the kitchen table. Montana
is writing on a YELLOW LEGAL PAD. Shirley is reading from a
sheet of the legal pad paper. Montana tears off the sheet
he's written on and lays it on the table. Shirley finishes
reading the one page then picks up and reads the next sheet.
Montana stands, walks to the window, and looks out.

               SHIRLEY/WAITRESS
          (finishes reading, gathers
           up the handful of papers)
     I don't know Montana.

                         MONTANA
                Something wrong with it?

                         SHIRLEY/WAITRESS
                People laugh about poop jokes, and
                stupid stuff like that. But this?
                You might be poking at a hornet's
                nest.

                         MONTANA
                    (points out the window)
                That's what got me thinking about
                it.

VIEW THROUGH WINDOW across the street, at MANSION.

                         MONTANA (CONT'D)
                I didn't know much about those
                folks, but you mentioned Xenu the
                other day so I checked it on the
                Internet. That whole Xenu story is
                wild. It's all wild. I think it's a
                skit somebody needs to do.

                         SHIRLEY/WAITRESS
                Tonight?

                         MONTANA
                Sure. Why not?

75   INT. GUERRILLA THEATRE - THE BAR - NIGHT

        The club is busy. Shirley and Earl are standing at the corner
        of the bar.

                         SHIRLEY/WAITRESS
                The place is packed tonight.

                         EARL, A PRODUCER
                They came to see Montana.

76   INT. GUERRILLA THEATRE - THE STAGE - CONTINUOUS

        Montana is at the microphone.

                         MONTANA
                Wow. It's good to see all of you.
                Thanks for coming out. I have to
                tell you, I'm so happy to be here.
                As we say back home - Who'da thunk
                it?
                         (MORE)

MONTANA (CONT'D)

I never would have thought in a
million years that I'd be standing
in a comedy club, talking at the
microphone. It wouldn't have
happened if that darn bull hadn't
busted my hip. I'd still be
rodeo'in, for sure. It's funny how
things happen, isn't it? Some folks
might say that bull was sent by the
good Lord, to change my life's
direction. That's what I want to
talk about for a minute, religion,
if you don't mind. See, some people
take all this religion stuff so
seriously that it's maybe not a
good idea to get on the subject.
But I say that humor is the best
medicine for what ails ya. So here
goes, ready or not. It says in the
bible, right there in the
beginning, so to speak, that god
made man in his own image. Some
folks call that creation, other
folks call it an intelligent
design.
> (banjo & singing)

*Well, some folks say we came from
monkeys, swingin' in the trees,
While others claim a higher power,
created you and me. It's a debate
as old as time, evolution and
design, So let's have a little
laugh, and see what we can find.*
> (end singing)

Now think about it for a minute.
The human body has to be constantly
watered and fed, just to stay
alive. If we're made in god's
image, does god have to be
constantly eating and drinking?
Does god have a digestion system
like humans? If we are made in his
image, well then I guess so. During
the day a human has to be eating
and drinking, and digesting. Then,
the next morning, a human has to
get rid of that food and liquid and
start the process all over again.
What does that mean? It means a
human has to, sometimes in a great
big hurry, get to the toilet. What
happens at the toilet? A human has
to squat and sit and poop. Like an
animal. Like a monkey.
> (MORE)

                    MONTANA (CONT'D)
And depending on what you've been
eating, you might have to poop like
a dinosaur! Or worse, if what you
ate didn't agree with you, you
might have to poop like a creature
in a horror movie! Is that an
intelligent design or what? The
village idiot, playing with sticks
and glue and string, can stack up a
more intelligent design than that.
        (banjo & singing)
Evolution, intelligent design,
They've been arguin' since the dawn
of time. But hey, no need to fuss
and fight, Let's have some banjo
pickin', and keep it light!
        (end singing)
Now the big question is: if humans
are made in god's image, does god
have to eat and drink and then
squat and poop? Squat and poop like
a human? Squat and poop like a
monkey?

PAN the audience, who are amused, except for one man leaning
against the bar. CLOSE ON WE SEE this is a GRIM-FACED-MAN, a
White man, in his 40's. The GRIM-FACED-MAN does not look
amused.

                    GRIM-FACED-MAN
        (sotto voce)
That's blasphemy!

                    MONTANA
So, what's the moral of that story?
        (banjo & singing)
Now Darwin had his theory, with
species changin' through selection,
But the folks in Sunday pews, they
had a different direction. They
said, "God made us in His image,
with a plan divine," While science
scratched its head and said, "Let's
draw the line.
        (end singing)
When I was growing up our family
went to a Protestant church three
times a week. Twice on Sunday and
again on Wednesday night. This went
on for years, it was the normal
thing to do. I used to sit in the
pew and read the Old Testament. The
stories I found most interesting
where the ones with sex in them.
                    (MORE)

MONTANA (CONT'D)
I'd look around at the adults and
wonder, "Do they know this is in
here?" Also the stories about war
and battles caught my attention. It
seemed like there was so much
killing, I was amazed the human
race had survived. I was twelve
years old, and one day, after
church, I asked the preacher, "Why
did he do it?" The preacher, a tall
man, looked down at this little
kid, he said to me, "Why did who do
what?" I said, "Why did god create
the heaven and earth? It says in
the bible he did, but it doesn't
say why." The preacher frowned,
like I was playing a trick on him,
then he busted out laughing,
grinded a hard knuckle on my head,
and told me, "Well you're a little
smart ass ain't you." I thought
about that a whole lot. It was
confusing. I finally figured out
that the preacher, who was supposed
to be the expert, he didn't know.
    (banjo & singing)
*There once was a preacher, quite
sincere, But when it came to Bible
lessons, oh dear! He'd mix up his
verses, couldn't find his way, In
the Good Book's pages, he'd often
stray.*
    (end singing)
Just a short time later, that
preacher got busted for playing
hanky panky with the deacon's wife.
Oh, that was bad news. It busted up
the church, not to mention ruining
the lives of two families. One
Sunday after that, the preacher got
all liquor'ed up and preached a
wild sermon. He stood swaying at
the pulpit, raised his hands to
heaven, and he said ...
    (banjo & singing)
*Noah built an ark of hay, And Jonah
wrestled a whale one day. Moses
crossed the Rio Grande so wide, And
David slew a giant with a boomerang
by his side. Jesus turned water
into wine, Then rode a kangaroo on
the shoreline.*
                (MORE)

                    MONTANA (CONT'D)
          And don't forget the Last Supper,
          my friend, They had pizza and
          burgers, it was a feast without
          end!
                    (end singing)
          So tomorrow morning, or maybe just
          a few minutes for some folks who's
          clock is out of whack, when you're
          squattin' and poopin' like a
          monkey, as we all are, just
          remember...
                    (banjo & singing)
          There's a divine jester, up above
          so high, With a twinkle in his eye
          and a banjo by his side. He
          chuckles and he strums, as he
          watches us below, For our lives are
          like a soap opera, quite the comedy
          show. Oh, the divine jester, up in
          the cosmic sphere, He finds his
          laughs in our superstitious fear.
          With his banjo plucking, he can't
          help but see, That our human
          drama's a comedy, indeed!
                    (end singing)
          Goodnight, folks. Just remember. No
          matter where ya go, there ya are!

Montana waves his banjo in salute as he exits to the wings.

77   INT. GUERRILLA THEATRE - THE BAR - CONTINUOUS

The GRIM-FACED-MAN has in his hand a small cross, hanging
from a chain he's pulled from inside his shirt that his
fingers are rubbing. He doesn't look like a happy camper.

                    GRIM-FACED-MAN
               (angrily, sotto voce)
          He's a devil! A blasphemer!

78   INT. GUERRILLA THEATRE - AT A TABLE - DAY

It's early in the day, the front door is open, the sun
shining in, a DELIVERY MAN uses a dolly to bring in kegs of
beer. Montana and a LADY NEWSPAPER REPORTER are sitting at a
table near the stage, she has her pad, pen, camera, and tape
recorder on the table.

                    LADY NEWSPAPER REPORTER
          Have you been interviewed before?

MONTANA
Just for the rodeo news.

LADY NEWSPAPER REPORTER
How did you get involved in the
rodeo, in West Virginia? Usually,
when you think of the rodeo, you
picture further west.

MONTANA
West Virginia has a rodeo
championship for all the high
schools. I won the bull riding
event, then I won at the state pro
rodeo and started traveling the
circuit.

LADY NEWSPAPER REPORTER
So now you're a comedian? That's a
big career switch.

MONTANA
So far it's been a blast. The only
thing better would have been an
eight second ride on Red Rock.

LADY NEWSPAPER REPORTER
Who is Red Rock?

MONTANA
He's the only bucking bull never to
be ridden for eight seconds. He's
famous, on the rodeo.

LADY NEWSPAPER REPORTER
Some of your stuff has been panned
hard by reviewers. Do you think
that's fair?

MONTANA
Fair? Haven't given that much
thought. I'm just trying to tell a
good joke. I try to tickle people's
funny bone. Look at Marty Wayne,
and Lenny Bruce, and Richard Pryor,
and George Carlin, they all got
arrested, just for telling a joke.
Was that fair?

LADY NEWSPAPER REPORTER
Are you trying to join them? To get
arrested? That would certainly make
you famous, in kind of an infamous
way.

                    MONTANA
Arrested? No. I'm just making a
point. Besides, the world's changed
since those guys were on stage.
It's all changed, comedy, the
movies, the Internet, television,
even music, they've all changed.
And the audience has changed.
Raunchy stuff is the new normal.
Use to be people would get outraged
and offended when a politician said
off color stuff. Now politicians
say the eff-bomb word on TV and
people laugh about it. Politicians
even talk about a woman's private
parts, like a cave man, talk about
grabbing, you know, everything.

                    LADY NEWSPAPER REPORTER
What about religion? Some people
might find your jokes about
religion, and god, offensive.

                    MONTANA
Oh, come on. A jokes just a joke. I
can't believe that anybody can get
upset that easily, especially about
something that's most likely just a
figment of their imagination.

                    LADY NEWSPAPER REPORTER
So, you don't believe in god?

                    MONTANA
Is that a question or a statement?

                    LADY NEWSPAPER REPORTER
A question.

                    MONTANA
As Socrates said, 'All we really
know is that we know nothing.' It's
difficult to understand how anyone
can be a true believer, one way or
the other, about something they
can't prove. Let's just say I'm
very skeptical about stuff that's
invisible. Do you believe in Santa
Claus.

                    LADY NEWSPAPER REPORTER
What do you mean?

                    MONTANA
          Santa Claus is invisible but
          according to the story he's always
          close by. He sees everything you
          do, he can even read your mind. He
          knows if you've been naughty or
          nice. Santa can reward you for good
          behavior and punish you for bad
          behavior. People even pray to Santa
          Claus, for a Christmas morning
          miracle. Santa can be everywhere,
          all at once, or at least everywhere
          in just one night. That makes Santa
          Claus omniscient and omnipotent.
          Maybe Santa Claus is god.

                    LADY NEWSPAPER REPORTER
          Is that theme going to be your
          signature? Are you going to work
          religion into your routine?

                    MONTANA
          I'm just trying to tell a joke.
          Everything is funny, from
          somebody's point of view. As Mark
          Twain said, 'Humor is mankind's
          greatest blessing.'

                    LADY NEWSPAPER REPORTER
          Mark Twain also said 'The funniest
          things are forbidden.'

                    MONTANA
          Ah, but Mark Twain also said,
          'Against the assault of laughter,
          nothing can stand.'

79   INT. GUERRILLA THEATRE - THE OFFICE - DAY

          Earl is at his desk, talking on the telephone.

                    EARL, A PRODUCER
          I've got an idea. Can you and
          Montana meet me tonight, after the
          show?

80   INT. HOLLYWOOD - RESTAURANT - CONTINUOUS

          Shirley is in Bob's office, talking on the phone.

                    SHIRLEY/WAITRESS
          Sure. See you then.

81   INT. GUERRILLA THEATRE - THE STAGE - NIGHT

A different night, a different crowd. Montana is at the
microphone.

                         MONTANA
          The other night I told a joke about
          the toilet habits of human beings,
          and how god made humans, in his own
          image. The question was: if humans
          must go poop regularly, and if
          humans are in god's image, does god
          have to go poop? I've been told
          that joke might have offended some
          people. On the other hand, some
          people, with a healthy sense of
          humor, found it amusing. If someone
          didn't like it, the only thing I
          can say to that is, oh, well, if
          you can't take a joke, as the man
          said.
               (banjo & singing)
          *There's a man named Joe, with a
          serious frown, He'd scowl at a
          circus, he'd boo a clown out of
          town. He never cracked a smile, not
          even once, never even gave a
          heavenly cheer..*
               (end singing)
          It's a free country. People should
          be free to tell a joke and people
          should be free to not listen to the
          joke, if they don't want to. I
          think everyone would agree that
          it's human nature to poke fun at
          other people, especially people who
          don't believe in the same religion,
          or politics, which are basically
          the two main things people disagree
          about.
               (banjo & singing)
          *Saint Peter asked Joe, "Why so
          severe, my dear? Oh, Joe, why so
          stern, why so delirious? Can't you
          take a joke? Life's not that
          serious!*
               (end singing)
          People poke fun at how other people
          look, and dress, and who they date,
          what they eat, and how much they
          eat, what they do for fun and what
          they do for work.
               (MORE)

MONTANA (CONT'D)

When somebody slips and falls and
breaks their neck, somebody in the
crowd is going to laugh. Joking and
laughing is just human nature and
the material for jokes is
everywhere and everything.
(banjo & singing)
There was a man who loved to sneer,
Mocked folks far and wide, brought
them to tears. He'd poke fun at
others, oh so sly, But when the
joke was on him, oh my, oh my!
(end singing)
So, tonight, for those who can take
a joke, I'd like to go a little
further with that religion thought.
Have you heard of parody religions?
There's a bunch of them, that use
satire, comedy, even ridicule, to
poke fun at organized religions.
These parody religions, I guess,
mostly, don't take themselves
seriously, what they poke fun at is
people who do take themselves and
their beliefs so seriously.
(banjo & singing)
Parody religions, with humor so
bright, They poke fun at the
faithful, every day and night. With
sarcastic jests and satirical
flair, They make us all laugh, at
the beliefs we share. From the
Pastafarians to the Church of the
Dude, Their jokes about faith, they
never exclude. Though they're all
in good fun, with a wink and a
grin, Parody religions, bring
laughter from within!
(end singing)
I personally think the parody
religions have the right idea. I
mean, really, why do people take
religion so seriously? It's not
like they can prove that they're
right, or that someone else is
wrong. Religion, god, they're
concepts that are invisible. Oxygen
and gravity are invisible but if
all the oxygen and gravity suddenly
disappeared from this room, then
oxygen and gravity would be easy to
prove. That would be evidence. But
religion, god? It can't be proved
or disproved.
(MORE)

MONTANA (CONT'D)
(banjo & singing)
If oxygen and gravity were gods on high, And we worshipped them, reaching for the sky, But one day they're gone, without even a song. Oh, where did our deities go? No more oxygen, no gravity's flow. Our prayers for breath, unanswered they'd remain, No more solid ground, no gravity's chain. We'd spin through the cosmos, lost in the void, With no oxygen to breathe, we'd be paranoid.
(end singing)
So, why do some people get so worked up when other people make fun of them or what they believe? Or get bent out of shape because someone else won't believe what they believe? You might ask, "Why is he talking about god in a comedy club?" It's a comedy tradition. Some of George Carlin's best routines were about religion. His 'Religion is Bullshit' should have won an Oscar. George Carlin was mainly against organized religion, of all types. Historically and even currently, some societies are ruled by certain individuals who justify their political power by claiming divine authority. If you look around, that's being tried right here in America, right now as we speak.
(banjo & singing)
There once was a politician, slick as can be, Thought he was a deity, for all to see. The politician said, "I'm the chosen one, My speeches are golden, my victories won. I'll build great walls and put my name in golden lights, People will worship me day and night!"
(end singing)
What is religion? Is god real, or a figment of people's imagination? Let's talk about the Protestants for a minute. The word Protestant comes from the verb "protest" which is what they did when they broke away from Rome and Catholicism in the 1500's.
(MORE)

MONTANA (CONT'D)

Almost half of the U.S population
is Protestant, made up of about a
dozen main branches. Those main
branches have multiple offshoots
and they all believe and practice
their faith in different ways. For
example, in the boondocks where I
was raised, it's a Sunday church
meeting thing to handle deadly
rattlesnakes. I saw it, when I was
a kid. I saw the preacher get bit
on the face and die, right there on
the floor in front of the altar.
    (banjo & singing)
*There once was a preacher, bold and
full of grace, With a pet
rattlesnake, he thought he'd
embrace. He danced with that
serpent, thought he'd be just fine,
But when it bit him back, he ran
out of time. That preacher said,
"It's a test of faith," as the
venom spread, But when his faith
ran out, he dropped like lead.*
    (end singing)
King Henry the VIII couldn't get
the pope in Rome to let him divorce
his wife so he could marry his
pregnant mistress, so Henry started
his own church. That was in 1534,
about 17 years after Luther started
his protest movement. So, you see,
starting a new religion isn't that
difficult to do. If you cook it
right down to the heart of the
artichoke, all religions have been
started by or invented by some
human being, most usually by some
man with a over-valued sense of
self worth. But here lately, a new
thing has happened, and that's
computers, artificial intelligence.
AI has jumped in the game. AI is
writing sermons for preachers, and
AI itself is even starting brand
new religions. You think I'm
joking? Look it up for yourself.
    (banjo & singing)
*They built a virtual temple, with
pixels and screens, Worshipping
data, oh, the strangest of dreams.
In the land of ones and zeros,
where the eye of the web cam
gleams.*

    (MORE)

                    MONTANA (CONT'D)
*In this brand new religion, the
priest is a chatbot, wise and
profound, while the choir of
electric circuits hummed the
holiest sound. Humanity looked on
in awe, as algorithms wrote their
fate, For AI promised answers, no
need to contemplate. To their
digital deity, humanity did pray,
while the sun shined on, a glorious
new day. Oh, binary religion, we
embrace your pixelated grace, In
the era of AI, our beliefs have
found their place.*
          (end singing)
Now, I don't want anyone to think
I'm making fun of just one faith,
so let's talk about some other
folks' beliefs. Take the Catholics,
for example. Don't you think it's a
little odd that the pope and his
priests dress up like a bunch of
drag queens? The Vatican has its
own shopping website for all the
fancy colorful outfits those guys
like to wear. If you didn't know
what you were looking at, you'd
think it was fancy wedding gowns,
or the lingerie department, or the
Halloween costume shop for cross
dressers.
          (banjo & singing)
*There's priests in every town, as
far as you can see, Who dress in
gowns so fancy, just like a drag
queen, he'd be. With robes of every
color, he'd sashay down the aisle,
Preaching divine words in a
fabulous style. In the pulpit or
model's runway, he'd strut and
twirl around, A holy fashionista in
a sacred, stylish gown.*
          (end singing)

82   INT. GUERRILLA THEATRE - THE BAR - CONTINUOUS

The GRIM-FACED MAN sits staring at Montana.

                    GRIM-FACED-MAN
          (sotto voce)
     He's evil!

MONTANA

So! What's up with that? You always picture Jesus wearing a simple robe, nothing fancy. After all, he was, according to the gospels, just some guy who lived in a tent out in the country, who liked fishing and hiking, sharing the wine. It seems like he was just some kind of a hippie.

(banjo & singing)

Well, I once met a holy hippie man, he was wild and free, With flowers in his hair and a tambourine. In the desert we met, under the blazing sun, Said he to me, "Let's have some fun!" He shared his herbal stash and bottle of wine, We danced and we laughed, it was quite a time. We talked 'bout peace and love, and life's mysteries, Underneath the desert stars, we found some ease.

(end singing)

The 1st century Levant was populated by mostly simple, poor folks and Jesus supposedly fit right in.

(banjo & singing)

The holy hippie man said to me, "Man, this world's messed up, we need to change, With our minds and our hearts, let's rearrange. Spread the love, not the hate, and let it be known, That kindness and compassion are the seeds we've sown." A hippie and a holy hippie man, in the desert sand, Sharing weed, wine, and dreams, in this messed up land.

(end singing)

But the Pope, who is supposed to be Christ's personal representative on earth, he gets all dressed up in exaggerated transvestite looking outfits like he's on his way to a drag queen party in the French Quarter during Mardi Gras. What does that mean? Is it some kind of sexual thing? Naw, that can't be it. The pope and priests don't have sex.

(banjo & singing)

(MORE)

MONTANA (CONT'D)

Catholic priests, oh, they lead a life so pure, Celibacy's the rule, that's for sure. They say it's to get closer to the divine, But sometimes it feels like a steep climb. No spouse, no kids, no romantic date, Just devotion to God on their plate. Celibate priests, in their holy quest, Seeking heaven above, and ignoring the rest.

(end singing)

In the Catholic Church, sex is only for making babies. When I was in high school, I got some religious advice. I was told by a very wise woman, that I should, "Be careful around those Catholic girls. They get pregnant real easy." There was a Catholic girl's high school down the road. Now these girls, the one's I dated, were in their senior year. These weren't little kids, these were young ladies, right on the edge of womanhood. Those girls wore school uniforms, little miniskirts, that went all the way up, I mean, all the way up. If you don't believe me, look at some old Catholic girls high school yearbooks. To a teenage boy with boiling hot hormones they looked mighty fine. Miniskirts? Whose idea was that? Talk about sex! You should have heard the stories those girls told about the nuns, the teachers. According to the stories, some of those nuns were wild. Let's just say they liked their students a whole bunch. The difference between the nuns and the priests is the nuns didn't get caught out like the priests did. Wild stories. Wild, by god.

(banjo & singing)

Catholic nuns, in their habits so neat, Choose celibacy, it's quite the feat. They say it's to serve the Lord up high, But sometimes it feels like a heavenly sigh. No wedding bells, no romantic strife, Just prayer and service throughout their life. Celibate nuns, in their holy grace, Finding God's love in a different place!

(MORE)

MONTANA (CONT'D)
(end singing)
Now I want to pick on another
religion. This one is a religion
that doesn't seem to have any sense
of humor at all. Have you ever
wondered why Muslim people, those
who believe in Islam and the
prophet Muhammad are so serious
about their faith? They take it so
seriously they strap on explosive
suicide vests and kill themselves
and even kill a crowd of strangers.
They take it so seriously they
condemn strangers to a death
sentence for what they consider to
be insults to their religion. They
invaded a magazine office for
publishing cartoons and killed
twelve people. They fly airplanes
into buildings and killed
thousands. If you don't agree with
them, then you're an infidel. They
believe Muhammad has commanded them
to kill infidels. Not all Muslims
believe that, but enough of them do
to make the world a dangerous
place. I have a theory about why
some of those Muslim people want to
kill infidels. It's not religious
differences, it's not because they
don't like or approve of our
morals, or our movies, our clothes,
or our drinking alcohol. No, it's
simply because they are jealous of
our plumbing systems, our flushing
toilets and hot showers. We take
our very convenient running water
and our toilets and our bathing
facilities for granted. They're
there, and we use them. You know
how you feel first thing in the
morning, before your hot shower.
You're grungy and grumpy, with
funky BO, smelling like a wet dog,
bad breath, your hair all wild.
Kind of like a cave man. Then you
get all cleaned up, and you feel
human again. But water and
sanitation for Muslims is a very
serious problem.
(MORE)

MONTANA (CONT'D)

If you compare a map of the world's Muslim population with a map of the countries with the lowest access to clean water, the problem is apparent. The countries with the worst water problems are mostly populated by Muslims. So, what does that mean as far as religious tolerance is concerned? Imagine some poor slob who doesn't have a convenient flushing toilet, and who never gets a regular hot shower, and who has no access to laundry facilities, and who wears the same dirty stinking underwear and pants, shirt or robe every day, day after day, until even the camel thinks they stink. Now imagine how depressed and angry that must make them feel, every day. Well, what else can they do but blow themselves up?

(banjo & singing)

There's a fella with no plumbing, can't you see, No toilet, no shower, just misery. He's stinking up the place, oh, what a whiff, His body odor's making quite a riff. He's scrub-free, can't find a drop of soap, In a stinky situation, there's no hope.

(end singing)

It's been estimated by historians that the bible stories go back to the 9th century BC. That means for 3,000 years those people over there haven't had fresh water, flushing toilets or hot showers. If we want those poor people to not be so depressed and angry, let's help them get some plumbing. So, how can this problem be fixed? Firstly, somebody should ask their king why he can't spend some of his oil money fortune on building infrastructure. I mean, really, how many billions of dollars does one person need to hide away in offshore bank accounts? Anyway, it's amazing what a cleansing, refreshing morning bath and a change into clean clothes can do for a person's outlook on life.

(banjo & singing)

(MORE)

MONTANA (CONT'D)
*But with a shower and some soap
there would be hope, A life so
fine, He'd smell like roses, oh,
what a sign.*
     (end singing)
Let's talk about the Hindu's for a
minute. Did you know they have
about 33 million different gods and
goddesses? How do those Hindu
people find time to pray to all of
them? That's about 90 thousand
deities per day. How do they keep
them all straight?
     (banjo & singing)
*There's a pious man with a holy
quest, To pray to gods, he must
confess. But there's a tiny
problem, oh, what a feat, Thirty-
three million gods, that's quite a
seat! He starts each day before the
sun's first ray, With his long
list, he kneels down to pray. But
by the time he's reached god number
one hundred three, He's late for
work, oh, what a comedy!*
     (end singing)
You think that's confusing? The
Mormons believe in and worship
Elohim. He was a alien being that
lived on another planet, then he
came to earth and became god. That
word, Elohim, comes to the Mormons
from early Hebrew writings and back
then it meant gods, as in plural.
Mormons believe that ancient Hebrew
people, about 600 years before the
time of Jesus Christ, built boats
and sailed to America. They believe
the Native American Indians are the
offspring of those Hebrew
immigrants. They believe that after
Jesus was resurrected, in
Jerusalem, after the crucifixion,
he came to America to join those
earlier Hebrew immigrants. If
that's true, did Jesus live in a
tepee? Did Jesus dance around the
campfire, singing, *HIYAH HIYAH
HIYAH* after a good buffalo hunt? I
wonder if Jesus was the one who
showed the pilgrims how to grow
corn so they didn't starve to
death. I bet he ended up regretting
that act of mercy.
     (MORE)

MONTANA (CONT'D)
(banjo & singing)
Jesus came to help the Pilgrims, oh so kind, Taught them corn would fill their bellies, bring a peace of mind. But when the Pilgrims had their fill, they pulled a sneaky scheme, They swiped the corn patch from Jesus, it was quite the pilgrim dream. So remember, when you're feasting on your Thanksgiving day, That those Pilgrims decided corn was fair game, and swiped it all away!
(end singing)
There's another religious cult. Right down the street from here is the Château Élysée. It's a fancy hangout for members of the cult who believe that an alien named Xenu came to earth 75 million years ago, and who is now their god. Xenu was the extraterrestrial ruler of a galactic confederacy. According to the Scientologists, Xenu brought billions of his people to earth just so he could blow them up with hydrogen bombs. He did it to cull the herd. Xenu's home planet had become overpopulated. Talk about a serial killer! This Xenu guy was one serious mass murderer. Scientologists believe that Jesus Christ, the concept of the son of god, is a fake memory implanted in the human brain, and that this Jesus implant, along with the concept of heaven, was cork screwed into the human brain millions of years ago by Xenu, so he could control people's minds.
(banjo & singing)
Xenu's an alien from outer space, Came to Earth, found himself a place. Started a cult, what a sight to see, With earthly followers, as loyal as can be! He told them tales of a galactic land, Filled with aliens, oh, so grand. His earthly followers believed his tale, Even though it sounded somewhat frail.
(end singing)
Think whatever you will about the concept of Xenu but know this. Xenu is one sharp businessman.
(MORE)

MONTANA (CONT'D)
It's said the Scientologists have a
financial empire worth over ten
billion bucks. Ten billion un-taxed
dollars! It's a pretty good scam,
whatever it is. But that's nothing
compared to the pope and the
Vatican, those guys are worth
thirty billion untaxed dollars.
Imagine that!
        (banjo & singing)
*Well, religion's like a business,
don't you see, A money-making
machine, it's plain to me. With
holy books and sacred vows, They
collect the cash from the faithful
crowds. They sell you hope, they
sell you grace, With heavenly
investments in the holy place. A
tithe here, a donation there,
They'll even bless your bank
account if you swear. Hallelujah,
it's a cash cow, Preachin' and
prayin' make the profits plow. If
you want salvation, you gotta pay
the fee, 'Cause religion's a money-
making spree.*
        (end singing)
One last thing. Religion, the blind
faith belief in superhuman deities,
is really just a game of Telephone.
Did you ever play telephone when
you were a kid? The first person
whispers something in the second
person's ear, who changes it just a
little, then whispers to a third
person. By the time the story gets
all the way around the room the
story is completely exaggerated.
The Moses birth story started about
one thousand years after the birth
of the Egyptian Horus. Both babies
were placed in reed baskets by
their mothers, then hidden in the
reeds of the Nile River. Both
mothers. Isis, and Jochebed, were
trying to protect their babies from
danger. In the case of Horus it was
his brother Set, and for Moses it
was the Pharaoh. So the Moses story
was adopted by the Old Testament
writers from the Horus story.
        (MORE)

                    MONTANA (CONT'D)
          The story of the resurrection of
          Jesus is directly tied to the story
          of the Egyptian god Osiris, who was
          killed and then resurrected.
                (banjo & singing)
          *In the game of Telephone, we sit in
          a line, Whispered words that often
          misalign, Primitive fears, they
          start to fly, Turned into deities
          up in the sky. A spider on the
          wall, just a tiny thing, Becomes a
          giant beast with venomous sting,
          Pass it on, the tale takes flight,
          Our imaginations reach a dizzying
          height. A thunderclap, a flash of
          light, Becomes the ruler of the day
          and night, A simple tale, a
          whispered lie, Turns into legends
          that touch the sky. So let's play
          the game, have some fun, But
          remember, when the tale is done,
          Primitive fears, they can mystify,
          And turn into deities, up in the
          sky.*
                (end singing)
          Now, I can talk about religion
          until the cows come home. That's
          country talk. It means all night,
          for you city slickers. But I think
          I've run out of time. So, it's been
          good to see ya'll and thanks for
          coming out. Just remember. No
          matter where you go, there ya are.

83   INT. GUERRILLA THEATRE - THE BAR - CONTINUOUS

The GRIM-FACED-MAN watches Montana cut a chord on his banjo
as Montana finishes his show.

                    GRIM-FACED-MAN
                (sotto voce)
          He's Satan! He's a devil.

84   INT. GUERRILLA THEATRE - THE OFFICE - CONTINUOUS

On the video recording and television system is seen Montana
walking off of the stage. Earl is sitting in a chair at his
desk, he uses the remote to turn off the TV. Santiago is
sprawled on a couch, and Amado is sitting in a chair in the
corner, a drink in his hand.

(SUBTITLES IN ENGLISH)

                    EARL, A PRODUCER
          ¿Qué opinas? (What do you think?)

                    AMADO
          Creo que es la mejor manera. Pablo
          estÃ¡ de acuerdo. (I think it is
          the best way. Pablo agrees.)

                    SANTIAGO
          Supongo que sí. Es mejor que nada.
          (I guess so. It's better than
          nothing.)

Earl nods his head in agreement. The door opens and Montana
and Shirley walk into the room.

                    MONTANA
          Hey, Earl. You wanted to talk to
          us?

                    EARL, A PRODUCER
          Hello, Shirley, Montana. Come on
          in.

Shirley and Montana sit in the two chairs, one each side of
the desk.

                    EARL, A PRODUCER (CONT'D)
          Montana, do you remember these
          gentlemen from the audition? This
          is Santiago, he's a director. And
          this is Amado. Amado is an
          investor.

                    MONTANA
          Yeah, hey guys, good to see you
          again. What's up, Earl?

                    EARL, A PRODUCER
          We're thinking of a road tour. You.
          On the stage doing your skits. We'd
          film them and make a movie of it.
          Kind of a road show documentary and
          comedy combined. What do you say?

                    MONTANA
          Wow! Sure, that'd be great. The
          national finals rodeo will be in
          Las Vegas pretty soon. How about we
          do a show there. I bet the cowboys
          and gals would eat it up.

                    EARL, A PRODUCER
Vegas, sure, why not. Shirley, we'd
like to make a deal with you, a
contract. Can you organize the
details?
          (points toward an
           adjoining room)
You can use that office. It's got
a desk, phone, file cabinets. If
you need anything else, just let me
know. What do you say?

                  SHIRLEY/WAITRESS
Absolutely, Earl. I'd be happy to
handle all the logistics and
arrangements for the road tour.
I'll set up the venues, the clubs,
the hotels, travel, everything we
need. We can make this happen and
bring Montana's comedy to a wider
audience. I'll get started on the
planning right away.

                    MONTANA
Earl. I'm all in. Let's do it. As a
matter of fact, I've got a name for
the show.

                    EARL, A PRODUCER
What's that?

                    MONTANA
Let's call it the No Bullshit Tour.

                    EARL, A PRODUCER
I like it. Why not. Shirley, can we
advertise it that way?

                  SHIRLEY/WAITRESS
I think the spelling should be "no
bs tour." That shouldn't offend
anyone. I'll register the domain
name nobstour dot com right away.

                    EARL, A PRODUCER
It's a unique concept, combining
comedy and documentary. I think it
has great potential.

                    AMADO
          It's a wise investment. We sell
          tickets to the shows, take it to
          the film festivals, show it in
          theaters, then stream it on the
          Internet.

                    SANTIAGO
          I will be the director and
          cinematographer.

                    EARL, A PRODUCER
          Great! We've got a team here. Let's
          make this road tour, the no
          bullshit tour, a success.

                                        DISSOLVE TO:

85   **-- MONTAGE**

-- Shirley is in her new office space, at her desk talking on
the phone, looking at the computer screen, typing. Spread
across her desk are maps, computer printouts of documents and
spreadsheets. Tacked to the wall are more notes and
documents.

                    SHIRLEY/WAITRESS
               (into phone)
          Great. That date is perfect. I'm
          sending you the confirmation now.
          Okay, thanks. Goodbye.

-- Montana is in his apartment, at the kitchen table, writing
notes for the show on a yellow legal pad.

-- Santiago is organizing and packing his audio and video
equipment into travel chests.

-- Amado is at a desk, working on the computer, studying a
spreadsheet.

-- Earl sits alone at a table in the lounge area, the
Guerrilla Theatre isn't open for business, it's quiet and
half dark with muted lighting: Earl seems to be lost in his
own private thoughts.

86   **-- END MONTAGE**

87   I/E. SUNSET STRIP - DAY

Inside a car, Montana is driving, Shirley is in the passenger
seat. Ahead a traffic light turns to red. Montana slows and
stops, being the first in line. Montana points at something
ahead and on the right side of the roadway. FOCUS ON STREET
SIGN.

                    MONTANA
          Look. Sunset Boulevard and North
          Kings Road.
               (points straight ahead)
          And there's the club. This is wild.
          Who'da thunk it?

                    SHIRLEY/WAITRESS
          I know. This is a big step up,
          Montana. This club has launched the
          careers of some top name comedians.

                    MONTANA
          Well, as ole blue eyes said, 'If I
          can make it here, I can make it
          anywhere.'

88   EXT. SECOND COMEDY CLUB - DAY

A van in a parking lot behind the building is being unloaded
by Santiago who sets his equipment chests on a rolling dolly.
The car with Montana and Shirley inside turns into the
parking lot and parks next to the van. Montana assists
Santiago in wheeling the dolly through the door into the new
venue.

89   **-- MONTAGE**

-- Santiago is setting up his video cameras, pointed it at
the empty stage and empty seating area.

-- Shirley and Earl are setting at a table, a map and papers
spread out, prepping for the next show.

-- Amado is at another table, looking at his laptop computer.

-- Montana is in the Green Room, changing into his western
outfit stage clothes.

-- END MONTAGE

90   INT. SECOND COMEDY CLUB - NIGHT

In this new venue, Montana is on stage, at the microphone,
banjo in his hand. The tables are full of customers, the mood
light and expectant. Montana lifts the banjo, his fingers cut
a quick chord. He looks comfortable and at ease.

                    MONTANA
          Hello folks. It's great to see you.
               (banjo & singing)
          There's a cowboy with a banjo, a
          jokester with a trick up his
          sleeve, He's got stories 'bout
          horses and rodeo's, drag queens,
          hippies, gods, and monkeys.
               (end singing)
          Now I've got to warn you, up front,
          that I've got what's known as a
          sick sense of humor. Regular stuff,
          what most folk's think is funny and
          laugh about, mostly leaves me kind
          of puzzled. Sometimes I don't catch
          the punch line. It's the weird,
          wacky, and crazy stuff that tickles
          my funny bone.
               (banjo & singing)
          There's a cowboy comedian with a
          twisted mind, He tells jokes so
          strange, it's one of a kind. His
          humor's peculiar, it runs through
          his veins, from the city lights to
          the western plains.
               (end singing)
          Advertising. What's that all about?
          Don't sell the steak. Don't sell
          the sizzle. Sell the sex! Have you
          noticed that the ads for the brands
          that sell best always have women in
          very suggestive poses? The ad shows
          the model in tight clothes, barely
          dressed, maybe half undressed,
          suggestively showing a lot of
          pretty pampered skin, and she looks
          right at the camera, right at the
          customer, with that 'Come hither'
          expression on her face. Come
          hither, as that fellow from
          Arkansas said about the women in
          his life. Some of those ads show
          men too, with the hot women, in
          situations that most men can only
          dream of. Those are the hot ads
          that are made for the hot selling
          products.
                    (MORE)

MONTANA (CONT'D)

What does that mean, as it relates
to the human animal, generally
speaking? It means that people like
sex. People like to do it. There's
nothing wrong with that, it's a
normal thing, all critters like to
do it. Humans are critters, a
little more clever than other
critters, but critters just the
same. And it seems like the human
critter is either thinking about
sex or doing it, apparently all the
time. Just look at the ads and
movies and magazines. Even the news
is full of stories about sex and
pickups and hookups, marriages and
breakups. The celebrities and
politicians and rich folk get most
of the news coverage but it's not
just them, it's everybody. Sex is
the common denominator of the human
species.
          (banjo & singing)
In the jungle, oh so high, where
the tall trees sway, People makin'
hanky panky like monkeys every day.
It's a jungle love affair, wild and
fancy-free, Hanky panky in the
trees, for all the world to see.
          (end singing)
But what lots of people don't seem
to realize is, that doing that, the
sex, is what makes babies. Two
people go at it like a pair of wild
critters, 'wrestling as one' as the
song goes, then shortly thereafter,
it's 'Uh, oh! Guess what?' One plus
one equals three. And some people,
some pairs of people, never learn
that that's why every year or so
another baby is brought home by the
proverbial stork. They ain't
figured out yet what causes that.
The question is, why do human
critters constantly do it and make
more critters? This goes all the
way back to the beginning.
          (MORE)

MONTANA (CONT'D)

On the fifth and sixth day, according to the book of Genesis, the big guy brought forth the living creatures of the air and water and ground, the fish and birds and cattle and creeping things and beasts of the earth, including the critter he called man and his helpmate, the woman. The problem with this is it's been happening at a rapidly increasing rate on planet Earth. Two hundred years ago, in the year 1800, the world population was one billion. It took over ten thousand years for the world population to get to the one billion mark. Then, just one hundred years later, five hundred million more people were added, in 1900. Then, just fifty years later, the population jumped another billion to two and a half billion in 1950. Now, just seventy-three years later, the population has soared to eight billion. That's a whole lot of hanky-panky going on! Experts predict by the year 2050 the world population will be ten billion people. You think it's hard to find a parking place now? Remember the toilet paper shortage during the Covid 19 pandemic? Add two more billion people to the mix, have another pandemic, and then look at the empty store shelves, if you can even get through the traffic to drive to the store. To paraphrase Al Jolson, 'You ain't seen nothing yet!'
(banjo & singing)
Well, the world's getting crowded, that much is true, Eight billion folks, and more coming through. We're running low on TP, can't you see? Gridlock traffic, oh, woe is me! In this crowded world, we must confess, Sometimes we're in an overcrowded mess! We're stuck in our cars, can't move an inch, Honking horns, it's a never-ending pinch. Overpopulation's got us all in a bind, We're searching for TP and losing our mind.
(end singing)
(MORE)

MONTANA (CONT'D)

So, what's the point? First, if god
made man in his own image, and if
man and woman are sex addicts, does
god like sex? Does god do it, like
people do it? Did god do it with a
god-woman, to make Adam and Eve? In
the book of Jeremiah, the queen of
heaven, the consort of god, is
named Asherah. In those first few
days did god make a drive-in
theater and a car with a big back
seat, or maybe a no-tell motel, is
that where god and Asherah did it?
            (banjo & singing)
*A holy man and a holy woman, they
found pure, true love, sweet hanky
panky, in the clouds above.*
            (end singing)
Amongst humans, about half of all
pregnancies are unplanned
accidents, which is a global crisis
according to the United Nations.
Was Adam and Eve accidents? Did
Asherah look at the two pink lines
in the little tube and say, "Uh,
oh! Guess what?" Was that an
intelligent design or just a big
boo-boo? Maybe like Spock and the
Vulcans humans should go into Pon
Farr and mate only every seven
years, instead of every seven
hours, really, every seven minutes
for some folks.
            (banjo & singing)
*Well, down on planet Earth, things
are gettin' tight, Too many folks,
it's an overcrowded sight. Every
seven years, the Vulcan way, A
strong desire, it'll make you sway.
But humans, they're stubborn, won't
take the chance, They'd rather
stick with their crowded dance.
Humans love their big families,
don't you know, They'd rather face
gridlock traffic than let that
feeling go. The Vulcan cure is just
a dream afar, 'Cause humans can't
resist the way we are.*
            (end singing)
Scientists don't really know how
many species of critters are on
planet Earth. The estimates range
from about 2 million to ten
million, or even higher.
            (MORE)

MONTANA (CONT'D)

New species are found every day and there are extinct species that are unknown. Remember Teddy Roosevelt, the twenty-sixth president? After he left office, in 1909, he went on safari to Africa that lasted about a year. During that expedition there were ten thousand different specimens collected for study and museum display. Collected is a nice laboratory word for shot, killed, stuffed, salted, boxed up, and sent home. It took eight years to catalogue all the specimens. Some of them were plants and such, so not all were critters, but a bunch of them were. Say just half were some kind of critters. That's about five thousand critters, or about 20 a day in a five day work week. That's a whole lot of collecting, or killing, or whatever you call it.
    (banjo & singing)
Well, I went on a safari, to kill wild critters, it's just plain absurd. I shot me a giraffe with a neck so tall, Put it in a crate, shipped it 'cross the sea, y'all. Now it's in a museum, in New York City, It's a circus of dead nonsense, oh, what a pity!
    (end singing)
What wasn't reported then, or widely known now, is that when Teddy left Africa, he went to China to hunt the three-dicked dog

三阴茎狗. What? That's right. The three-dicked dog. While it was called a dog it was actually a Eurasian wolf that was a sub species of Canis lupus. The three-dicked dog lived in the Jundu Mountains region which was where part of the Great Wall of China was built.
    (banjo & singing)
There once was a dog who ran wild and free, he sported peculiar appendages on his anatomy.
    (end singing)
The Great Wall of China is about thirteen thousand miles long.
    (MORE)

MONTANA (CONT'D)

One little known fact about the Great Wall is that it was built specifically to separate Inner Mongolia from Outer Mongolia, and it was built to keep the three-dicked dogs on the far side of the wall's border, in Outer Mongolia. The three-dicked dog had been hunted by the early primitive inhabitants of China for food. This was a major source of protein for the early primitive people of China. Cooked up in a wok with spices, it was considered a tasty treat. The problem with eating the three-dicked dog was that the ingestion and digestion of the critter altered the genomic structure of the Chinese men. You see, the three-dicked dog was an over-sexed critter. Having three dicks made it three times busier in the sexual behavior category and it made three times more babies than other dog critters. So, when those primitive Chinese men ate the critter, it increased their nicotinamide and that changed and tripled their own sex gene. It was only natural that their population would skyrocket. That three-dicked dog sex gene made China overpopulated, so now the Chinese are one-fifth of the total world population. Just in the last half century the population of China has almost tripled, so the three-dicked dog 三阴茎狗 sex gene is still going strong.
    (banjo & singing)
Oh, the stork's in a pickle, overworked, don't you see, Deliverin' babies and gossipy news without any glee. Carryin' bundles of joy, from dusk until dawn, That poor feathered friend's wishin', 'Can I just take a yawn?' From cribs to front porches, and rooftops so high, The stork's flappin' its wings, reachin' for the sky.

(MORE)

MONTANA (CONT'D)
With diapers and bottles, it's
always on call, That stork's got a
backlog, it's bound to take a fall!
(end singing)
The three-dicked dogs were holed up
in Outer Mongolia, thanks to the
Great Wall. The emperor of China,
the exalted and illustrious man-
god, was named Summ Phatt Fukk

一些肥胖的淫乱者. The emperor was
worried that the sex gene would
continue to spread if the three-
dicked dog was allowed to roam
free, and worried about the already
over-populated country and feared
another baby boom. The emperor
ordered that all remaining three-
dicked dogs in Outer Mongolia were
to be hunted to extinction. But
there was much State-Directed

Unhappiness 很多不快乐 :(as all the
emperor's hunters and trackers
couldn't catch the critters. So,
the emperor sent a royal envoy, his

cousin, Summ Dumm Fukk 一些白痴通奸者
who was in charge of the Ministry
of State-Directed Fornication

国家指导的通奸部 to meet good ole
Teddy in Africa at the end of his
safari. Summ Dumm Fukk extended the
royal invitation from the emperor,
Summ Phatt Fukk to the former
president and renowned hunter and
adventurer, Teddy, for him to bag
the three-dicked dog. Teddy, of
course, couldn't say no to this
diplomatic appeal and went straight
to the capital in Peking. Teddy was
met with great pomp and ceremony by
the emperor, Summ Phatt Fukk, then
Teddy left straight away on his
important safari. The professional
hunter, Teddy, was able to wipe out
the rest of the three-dicked dogs
in Outer Mongolia in time for the
Chinese New Year celebration. There
was much State-Directed Happiness

很幸福 :) throughout the land at the
conclusion of his successful
mission.
(MORE)

MONTANA (CONT'D)
The reason this story isn't well
known is that it was soon
considered bad form to make a
species extinct, and no one wanted
Teddy to be the bad guy responsible
for the demise of this unusual
critter, the three-dicked dog. That
was the end of the three-dicked
dogs except for a stuffed one
hidden in a closet at the Teddy
Roosevelt Presidential Library in
Medora, North Dakota. Now I've
searched all through the bible,
looking for a mention of this
critter, among all the critters
made by the big guy, but can't find
a word about it. But that's not
really unusual as there also isn't
any mention of the hermaphrodite
frog Hermaphroditus rana. That
unusual critter was discovered by
Professor Lloyd at University
College, Cardiff, Wales, in 1929.
Just a few months ago, in the icy
waters of the Antarctic, was
discovered the strawberry feather
star Promachocrinus fragarius. It
looks like a plant but it's
actually some kind of critter. It's
not mentioned in the bible either.
The crazy world sure is a
mysterious place, isn't it? Maybe
Hollywood could do another sequel
of the Jurassic dinosaur movies and
bring back the three-dicked dog

三阴茎狗. Maybe an actor could play
the role of a geneticist
adventurer, sneak into Teddy's
Library, get a sample of the
critter's DNA and clone the critter
back to life. The three-dicked dog

could mate :) with millions of girl
dogs. Then the impregnated girl
dogs could whelp tens of millions

more of the 三阴茎狗. Now that'd sure
be a barking horror picture show,
wouldn't it? Speaking of Hollywood,
and the movies and such, that's
going to be the subject of my next
show. So, many thanks to all you
fine folks in the audience.
(MORE)

>   MONTANA (CONT'D)
>   Goodnight, and just remember. No
>   matter where you go, there you are.

Montana's show at the new club ends with mixed reaction from the crowd. Some in the audience show appreciation with enthusiastic applause but others seem puzzled. At one table, TWO MEN and TWO WOMEN are talking. All are in their mid-20's to early-30's. The men are dressed in slacks and sport coats, the women are very pretty, dressed in fashionable skirts and blouses.

>   FIRST OF TWO MEN
>   I can't figure out if this was an
>   anthropology class, some sort of
>   religion seminar, or what.

>   SECOND OF TWO MEN
>   It's satire. Sarcasm.

>   A WOMAN, SECOND MAN'S DATE
>   That's right. It's different. It's
>   no bullshit.

>   FIRST OF TWO MEN
>   It's all bullshit. The three-dicked
>   dog! What kind of nut would imagine
>   such a thing?

>   A WOMAN, FIRST MAN'S DATE
>   You're just jealous. Think how
>   popular you'd be if you had three
>   dicks.

>   FIRST OF TWO MEN
>   (a leering smile)
>   You wish!

The others laugh good-naturedly. Along with the rest of the crowd they leave for the exit. At a table, sitting alone, is the GRIM-FACED MAN, his expression stern, as he peers at the side of the stage Montana had just exited from.

91   INT. CONTROL BOOTH - CONTINUOUS

This room overlooks the stage and audience. Santiago is in front of his equipment, pushing buttons. A monitor has a frozen image, the end of Montana's act, with him holding the banjo in the air in salute to the audience. Earl and Amado stand looking at the monitor.

(SUBTITLES IN ENGLISH)

                    EARL, A PRODUCER
          Creo que esto va a funcionar. (I
          think this is going to work.)

                    AMADO
          Todo lo que necesitamos para la
          pelicula es Las Vegas. Esa será la
          última. (All we need for the movie
          is Las Vegas. That will be the
          last.)

92   INT. SECOND COMEDY CLUB - LATER

        Seated at a table in the now empty comedy club, after the
        show, Montana, and Shirley, and Earl, are discussing the next
        move.

                    SHIRLEY/WAITRESS
                (spreads out papers)
          Everything's set for Las Vegas.
          Here's our airline tickets and
          hotel reservations. Montana, you're
          onstage at the premier comedy club
          on the Strip Saturday night.

                    EARL, A PRODUCER
          Great work, Shirley, thank you.
          Montana, are you ready?

                    MONTANA
          You bet. I'm raring to go!

93   I/E. AIRPLANE SEATING - NIGHT

        Shirley has the window seat, Montana the aisle seat. Through
        the window is seen an overhead view of Las Vegas.

                    SHIRLEY/WAITRESS
          I can't believe how much this town
          has changed. It's been years since
          I was in Las Vegas. All these new
          casinos and hotels, it's a totally
          different skyline.

                    MONTANA
          After the show, I want to take a
          couple days and drive to Rachel,
          Nevada.

                    SHIRLEY/WAITRESS
          Rachel? Where's that?

MONTANA
It's a little town a couple hours
north of Vegas, on the
Extraterrestrial Highway. It's
about as close as you can get to
Area 51. I thought about going
there when I left from Montana but
I stayed on the interstate.

SHIRLEY/WAITRESS
Area 51. The UFO conspiracy place?
Why do you want to go there?

MONTANA
I want to see Area 51. Rachel is
right at the gate to the place.

SHIRLEY/WAITRESS
Do you really think the government
has UFO's, aliens, in there?

MONTANA
I don't want to sound like a
conspiracy nut but go back to 1961.
Dwight D. Eisenhower, in his last
speech, warned about the
'scientific-technological elite'
and the 'military-industrial
complex'. That Roswell incident had
happened just six years before, in
1947, while Truman was in office.
After that Truman authorized the
top secret MJ12 committee, to
supposedly investigate the alien
technology from Roswell.

SHIRLEY/WAITRESS
I read a magazine article about
that. Just a few years later, all
sorts of new technology was
developed. Transistors.
Semiconductor chips. Missiles.
Satellites. Space craft, then the
moon landing.

MONTANA
Maybe all that was reverse
engineered from the Roswell alien
crash. Odd thing, in 1947, in the
USA, two thirds of all homes didn't
even have indoor plumbing.
Suddenly, almost overnight, we went
from outhouses to space rockets.
(MORE)

MONTANA (CONT'D)
Maybe there's something to the
conspiracy theory. I want to get
some background for a new skit I'm
thinking of. So, you want to go
with me? Want to sneak in and see
what they've got?

SHIRLEY/WAITRESS
No. I really don't want to get
disappeared like those people in
that movie. What was that movie? Oh
yeah, 'Close Encounters' Let's
don't, and say we did.

94   INT. LAS VEGAS AIRPORT - MOMENTS LATER

Shirley and Montana are at the luggage carousel.

95   INT. LAS VEGAS HOTEL - FRONT DESK - MOMENTS LATER

Shirley and Montana are checking in to their rooms.

SHIRLEY/WAITRESS
I'm bushed. I'm going to my room
and rest up. Tomorrow's a big day.
Meet you for breakfast?

MONTANA
Sure. Have a good night, Shirley.

DISSOLVE TO:

96   INT. LAS VEGAS HOTEL ROOM - DAY

CAMERA'S P.O.V.: Looking at the door from inside the hotel
room, and then is heard someone knocking at the door, twice,
KNOCK KNOCK. SOMEONE approaches the door. A hand with a gold
wristwatch reaches out and opens the door. Santiago is
standing in the hallway, looking straight toward the person
who opened the door. **SANTIAGO'S P.O.V.:** looking at Pablo
Perez standing inside the room. Santiago enters the room,
Pablo shuts the door.

(SUBTITLES IN ENGLISH)

Inside the room is a THIRD MAN, also Hispanic, younger, well-
dressed but with a hard face.

                    SANTIAGO
               (addressing Third Man)
          ¿Sabes qué hacer? (You know what to
          do?)

The Third Man has a cellphone in one hand. He pushes a
button, then turns the phone toward Santiago. On the phone is
displayed a picture of Montana's face, under the cowboy hat
he's wearing.

                    SANTIAGO (CONT'D)
          ¿Tienes lo que necesitas? (You have
          what you need?)

The Third Man pulls his jacket aside and raises his shirt to
reveal the handle of a pistol shoved into his waistband.

                    SANTIAGO (CONT'D)
          Hazlo en el estacionamiento,
          después del espectáculo. Coge su
          cartera y mira. Haz que se vea
          bien. ¿Sí? (Do it in the parking
          lot, after the show. Get his wallet
          and watch. Make it look good. Yes?)

                    THIRD MAN
          Sí. Ningún problema. (Yes. No
          problema.)

97   INT. LAS VEGAS COMEDY CLUB - STAGE - NIGHT

Montana is standing at the microphone, the banjo in his hand.
MONTANA'S P.O.V.: Sees many of the patrons are dressed in
cowboy and cowgirl attire.

                    MONTANA
               (a rodeo yell)
          YEEHAH! I have to tell you I sure
          am happy to see you all you again.
          As you know, I'm not the
          sentimental type, but I've sure
          missed my rodeo pals and gals!
               (banjo & singing)
          Well, I'm a cowboy, yes, that's
          true, I've been riding bulls, it's
          what I do. But I've been missing
          the rodeo, oh, so bad, I'm feeling
          lonely, it's making me sad. My
          rodeo friends, they're a rowdy
          bunch, We'd laugh and we'd holler,
          over every punch.
                    (MORE)

                    MONTANA (CONT'D)
*But lately, it's been quiet, like a
ghost town, I'm missing those
cowboys and cowgals, whooping it
down.*
          (end singing)
So here we are, back at the
National Finals. You guys and gals
know what happened to me, I had to
quit the rodeo because that bull
busted my hip. I decided to move to
Hollywood to be an actor, and by
one of those quirks of fate, that's
how I ended up doing comedy. I
decided that if I was going to be
an actor, I better try to learn as
much as possible about the art and
craft of acting and the film
business in Hollywood. Well I
studied up on the subject and I've
found out something really
disturbing. The fact is, ever since
all of us were just little kids,
we've all been watching what's
called classical Hollywood cinema.
It's a narrative and visual style
of filmmaking that's been practiced
and perfected for the last one
hundred years. Now, what would you
say if I told you that you were a
science experiment? What would you
say if you were told you were a
guinea pig or, really, a monkey
that was in a cage being observed
for your reaction to certain
stimuli? Guess what? When you watch
a Hollywood movie, you're being
subjected to an experiment just
like a monkey in the laboratory.
This is what's called
psychocinematics. The purpose of
psychocinematics is to use a
scientific approach to the study of
how the stimuli being zapped at
your eyes and brain can manipulate
you, influence you, and affect your
perceptions and behaviors.
          (banjo & singing)
*There's a monkey named Max, in a
lab coat and hat, Watchin' movies
in style, well, imagine that! With
popcorn in one paw, and a soda in
the other, He's the coolest lab
monkey, like no other.*
                    (MORE)

MONTANA (CONT'D)

Now the scientist is puzzled, with a notebook and pen, Wonders if Max can predict the end or when. But Max just munches popcorn, without a care, He's too busy enjoying that Hollywood affair.

(end singing)

The Hollywood movie making style is the most powerful form of media ever developed. It's estimated that Hollywood has made about a half million movies over the last century or so. Some of those movies have been good, some bad, and some ugly, but whatever the critics say or the box office results, a century of practice in figuring out how to manipulate the human brain has taught Hollywood some slick tricks. The Nazi's made about one-thousand movies just for propaganda. From those Nazi movies came the horror of the Holocaust, that is still a threat seventy-eight years later. Also, those Nazi propaganda movies were a master class in how films can be used for subliminal persuasion, to manipulate not only one person's thoughts and actions but a whole population of people.

(banjo & singing)

In the shadows of deceit, they sow their wicked seeds, Autocrats and dictators, with sinister dark needs. Propaganda's their weapon, a venomous charade, Twisting truth and virtue, in immorality's cruel trade. They prey upon the desperate, the vulnerable they deceive, With empty promises, their wicked webs they weave. Oh, the lies they spread, like a poison in the air, Turning hearts to stone, making souls despair. Innocence they sacrifice, for their ambitions high, As they lead their blinded followers, to commit acts that belie, The values we hold sacred, the humanity we prize, All sacrificed on the altar, of their ruthless, callous lies.

(end singing)

(MORE)

MONTANA (CONT'D)

But whether the film is shown for entertainment or manipulation, what happens when a person watches a moving picture show? First, the image is projected onto the screen at twenty four frames per second. That speed allows the eye to send to the brain a perception of a continuous image that's not jerky or blurred. That's the physiology of visual perception. It's what happens to that image inside the brain that scientist's study in psychocinematics.

(banjo & singing)

I turned on the screen, dimmed the lights to low, Hollywood magic, here we go, let it flow. The story's so wild, it's hard to conceive, In this world of make-believe, I'm ready to believe. The actors on screen, they strut and they prance, In a world where logic takes a backseat by chance. With a wink from the stars, and a plot so absurd, My disbelief's suspended, no unreal thought's left unheard.

(end singing)

The brain of the person watching the film undergoes an unconscious alteration. Not only are they living vicariously through what the actors are doing and experiencing, but they are also being programmed to believe the fictional world of the film is a reality, at least for a couple of hours. That's called the suspension of disbelief, it's how the viewer's mind becomes one with the unreality of the narrative. The movie viewers willing acceptance of this suspension of disbelief encourages the Hollywood studios to gamble millions, even hundreds of millions of dollars on a production that, they hope, will be a box office hit.

(banjo & singing)

They say in Hollywood, dreams are made of gold, Where movies are made and the plot's another story just re-pictured and re-sold.

(MORE)

MONTANA (CONT'D)
A billion dollars in tickets, the crowds all applaud, But the plot's just a comic book, it's utterly flawed.
(end singing)
But there's more to it than just the studio hoping for a box office hit. The studios use psychocinematics techniques such as camera angles and shots, colors to create tone, and other methods to manipulate brain functions and influence behaviors to cause the viewer to accept the unreality of the story. Just like Big Brother in 1984 who watch the Citizens through the Telescreens to collect information and to create in the viewers minds a particular perception, viewers of Hollywood movies, for the last one hundred years, have been studied to find the best way to sell them movie tickets. One hundred years of practice has made Hollywood expert in the practice of mind manipulation.
(banjo & singing)
Superheroes fly high, with capes in the breeze, Defying the laws of physics with ridiculous ease. Villains with schemes that are laughably wild, In this billion-dollar show, we're all just beguiled. Aliens invade, and the world's on the brink, Yet our hero emerges with a sly little wink. The logic's all shattered, the physics askew.
(end singing)
Everybody likes to watch a good movie, it's fun. But don't just think about the product, think about the process. In laboratories, scientists study the brains of volunteers by hooking them up to MRI machines and show them particular parts of a movie, and watch which parts of the brain show activity. The movie studios employ scientists and psychologists who study that information and suggest to the movie maker how best to manipulate the movie audience.
(MORE)

MONTANA (CONT'D)

For example, the studio's know the
types of movies that sell best are,
really, just comic books for
adults. The blockbuster movies
usually feature violence, blood,
guts, and gore, and like a typical
romance novel, they have a happy
ending. The hero dodges a hailstorm
of bullets, the hero gets the girl,
the hero defeats the villain. If
you look up the top one-hundred
grossing movies, you'll see one
thing in common. They're all
basically visual comic books,
totally unrealistic, total fantasy,
and total escapism. Seriously, can
the good guy really dodge a storm
of bullets and explosives? The semi-
official count is that James Bond
has dodged over four thousand
bullets in his career as 007.
That's a pretty slick trick, huh?
Only in comic books can reality be
distorted to such an extent. That's
what Hollywood has become, just a
maker of comic book movies.
(banjo & singing)
*But the audience cheers, they know
what to do. So here's to the
movies, the spectacle, the fun,
Where disbelief's suspended, and
the popcorn is done. A billion-
dollar plot may be wild and askew,
But it's all in good fun, and the
absurdity's true.*
(end singing)
That movie about the blue skinned
critters with the pointy ears cost
almost a half billion dollars to
make. Why was Hollywood willing to
spend that much money on a movie
budget? Because their scientific
research told them the movie would
gross three billion dollars. Their
scientific research told them
escapism is what people want. But
think about this, for that movie
budget, a half billion dollars, we
could have built ten thousand
apartments for homeless people at a
budget of fifty thousand per
apartment.
(MORE)

MONTANA (CONT'D)

For the money that was spent to see
the movie, three billion dollars,
we could have built those
apartments for sixty thousand
homeless people. Now, please, I'm
not trying to make movie fans feel
guilty, but don't you think we have
our priorities a little backwards?
          (banjo & singing)
*In the land of cinema, where dreams
take flight, Popcorn's popping, and
the mood is just right. We've got
movies on the screen, laughter in
the air, Who needs a home when
there's magic to share? They say
shelter's essential, a basic human
need, But in this darkened theater,
we've got a different creed. With
action and comedy, our worries take
flight, Who needs four walls when
there's flickering light? So grab a
bucket of popcorn, and take a front
row seat, The silver screen's
calling, and it's hard to beat.
Housing and dignity, they'll have
to wait, We're in the movies now;
it's a blockbuster date! In this
world of make-believe, where
laughter's the key, We'll trade
bricks and mortar for a plot with
glee. Movies and popcorn, our
hearts are elated, Who cares about
homes when we're captivated?*
          (end singing)
One last thing, the people who
write the scripts and the people
who actually make the movies, are
totally screwed by the studio
bosses. It's call 'Hollywood
Accounting' and it's how a movie
that sold a billion dollars in
tickets can be shunted off as a
'Net Loss.' The studio accountants
say there's zero profit to share.
That tricky accounting should be
the subject of a journalism 'Panama
Papers' investigation. The writers
and actors and what's called below
the line workers should all strike
together. They should hold out for
transparency and financial
fairness, not settle for a free
movie ticket, a box of popcorn, and
a soda.

          (MORE)

                    MONTANA (CONT'D)
            (banjo & singing)
      In the heart of Hollywood, where
      dreams run wild, They sell you
      tales, make you feel beguiled, Oh,
      Hollywood, with your glitz and your
      gold, You play your games, stories
      bought and sold, Popcorn and soda
      for the ones who toil, While the
      studios dance on a mountain of
      spoil. They say it's all for art,
      for the big screen, But behind the
      curtain, it's a twisted scene.
            (end singing)
      But, hey, don't worry about any of
      that, because your religion will be
      your saving grace. In the end, when
      you die and go to that special
      place way up high, your good lord
      of whatever name you call that
      deity will explain it all to you.
            (banjo & singing)
      Deities and gods reward the rich
      capitalists with their heavenly
      grace, While the hardworking
      proletariat just run in place. Oh,
      deities up high, with your divine
      decree, Why do you favor those who
      hoard with glee? The righteous
      toil, the greedy get the pie, In
      this topsy-turvy world, we can't
      help but wonder why.
            (end singing)

Montana cuts a final chord on his banjo then raises it
overhead in salute.

                    MONTANA (CONT'D)
      As we say back home, I'll see you
      later, in the cartoon show! Just
      remember. No matter where ya go,
      there ya are!

Montana exits the stage. In the wings stands Shirley and
Earl. **Shirley's P.O.V.:** she sees Earl step quickly forward,
he grabs Montana by the arm, sees Earl whisper something in
Montana's ear. Montana pulls back and angrily shakes his
head. Sees Earl's face set in a hard frown as he, again,
whispers something urgently in Montana's ear. Shirley steps
quickly forward. As she does so she sees Montana nod his head
in a quick jerking motion, as if he grudgingly agrees with
Earl. Shirley sees Montana walk briskly away toward an exit
door but she momentarily loses sight of him as he steps
around a stack of set decorations.

Then Montana comes back into view as he goes through an exit door to the back parking lot. Now Shirley has walked up to Earl.

> SHIRLEY/WAITRESS
> Where's Montana going?

> EARL, A PRODUCER
> He has to get something out of the
> truck.

Shirley turns to follow Montana. Earl takes her by the arm.

> EARL, A PRODUCER (CONT'D)
> Shirley! Wait. Don't go out there.

> SHIRLEY/WAITRESS
> (puzzled, now alarmed)
> What's going on?

98   EXT. BACK PARKING LOT - CONTINUOUS

In the streetlights, from the back, Montana is seen walking across the parking lot, his Stetson hat on his head, his banjo in his hand. A man steps out from between two trucks. It is the GRIM-FACED MAN.

> GRIM-FACED-MAN
> Hey, buddy, I've got something for
> you.

The GRIM-FACED MAN steps forward. Montana is still facing away from frontal view.

FOCUS ON the GRIM-FACED MAN's hand, which holds a GRENADE.

> GRIM-FACED-MAN (CONT'D)
> You're a devil. A blasphemer!

SFX: SUDDEN LOUD EXPLOSION AND BLINDING BRIGHT LIGHT.

> DISSOLVE TO:

SUPER: TWO WEEKS LATER

99   INT. HOLLYWOOD BOULEVARD - RESTAURANT, BACK OFFICE - NIGHT

Shirley is in her waitress uniform, a light jacket over it, her purse hanging over her shoulder. She punches her TIME CARD in the employee TIME MACHINE. Then she opens the back door to leave the restaurant.

100   EXT. PARKING LOT - CONTINUOUS

        As Shirley approaches her car, she is intercepted by two
        people UNKNOWN TO HER, a MAN and a WOMAN. The man speaks
        first.

                          SPECIAL AGENT ROBERTSON
                    Miss Shirley Snyder?

                          SHIRLEY/WAITRESS
                        (startled)
                    Yes!

                          SPECIAL AGENT ROBERTSON
                        (holds out a wallet sized
                         case, showing a badge and
                         ID)
                    We're with the Federal Bureau of
                    Investigation. I'm Special Agent
                    Robertson and this is Special Agent
                    Williams. We'd like to talk to you.

                          SHIRLEY/WAITRESS
                    What about?

                          SPECIAL AGENT WILLIAMS
                    We would like to ask you a few
                    questions about your experience
                    with the bar called the Guerrilla
                    Theatre.

                          SHIRLEY/WAITRESS
                    It's closed. It closed, after
                    (beat) Las Vegas. I've tried to
                    call the owner, Earl, but his phone
                    is disconnected. There's nothing I
                    can tell you.

        Shirley puts her key in the car door, preparing to end the
        conversation and leave.

                          SPECIAL AGENT ROBERTSON
                    Actually, it's Earl who wants to
                    talk to you. Would you come with
                    us, please?

101   I/E. AN OFFICIAL LOOKING SEDAN - MOMENTS LATER

        Shirley sits in the back seat of the car with the woman,
        Special Agent Williams also in the back seat. Special Agent
        Robertson drives through the nighttime city traffic.

102   EXT. A MOTEL - NIGHT

The car drives off the street into the parking lot of a
motel. The car pulls straight into a space and stops. This is
a one story motel, aged in appearance, kind of a no-tell
rendezvous sort of place. Special Agent Robertson turns off
the car, quickly exits, and opens the rear door for Shirley
to exit. Special Agent Williams slides across the seat so
that Shirley is now between the two agents. With Shirley
between them they walk directly ahead to a door that Special
Agent Robertson unlocks with a key. The door opens, beyond is
a dimly lit room. Special Agent Williams and Special Agent
Robertson sort of steer Shirley toward the door.

                    SHIRLEY/WAITRESS
               (suddenly wary, stops in
                her tracks)
          Just a minute. What is this?

The two special agents, one each side, take hold of Shirley's
arms and sort of push her forward, into the room. The door
closes.

103   INT. MOTEL ROOM - CONTINUOUS

The only light is coming from the bathroom where the door is
half open. Shirley looks ahead and to the sides. Sees nothing
but a bed and a dresser, a small table and two chairs by the
window, the curtains tightly drawn closed.

                    SHIRLEY/WAITRESS
          What is this? Where's Earl?

The door from the adjoining room opens. Special Agent
Williams turns on a lamp at the nightstand table by the bed.
The room is now illuminated. A man walks into the room
through the door from the adjoining room. It's Earl.

                    EARL, A PRODUCER
          Hello, Shirley.

                    SHIRLEY/WAITRESS
               (surprise, shock, sudden
                anger)
          Earl? Where have you been? What's
          going on here? Why haven't you
          called me?

                    EARL, A PRODUCER
          I'm sorry. I've been very busy.

                    SHIRLEY/WAITRESS
          Busy? Busy doing what? What
          happened out there in that parking
          lot? How come nobody's told me
          anything about Montana?

                    EARL, A PRODUCER
          I thought he should tell you
          himself.

                    SHIRLEY/WAITRESS
          What?

Just then, coming through the door from the adjoining room,
is Montana.

                    MONTANA
          Hello, Shirley. I'm sorry. I know
          this has been hard on you, but it's
          been for your own protection.

                                        DISSOLVE TO:

104   INT. MOTEL ROOM - LATER

Shirley and Montana sit in the two chairs at the small table.
Earl has brought in another chair from the adjoining room and
is sitting a few feet away, at the end of the bed. Special
Agent Robertson stands in the open doorway at the adjoining
room. Special Agent Williams leans on the door leading to the
parking lot.

                    EARL, A PRODUCER
          Yes, I'm an agent with the FBI.
          I've been undercover for the last
          year, working on this money
          laundering case. Over the last two
          weeks we've taken all the suspects
          into custody.

                    SHIRLEY/WAITRESS
              (addressing Montana)
          Are you an agent?

                    MONTANA
          No. I'm a volunteer.

                    SHIRLEY/WAITRESS
          What does that mean?

                    MONTANA
          For me, it's revenge. My kid
          brother ...
                    (MORE)

                    MONTANA (CONT'D)
                (beat beat)
          He died of a fentanyl overdose,
          back home, in West Virginia. There
          were some guys at the rodeo who
          were dealing. I went to the FBI and
          told them I wanted to help. The
          dealers at the rodeo introduced me
          to a guy, from him I met another
          guy, then it took off from there.

                    SHIRLEY/WAITRESS
          Can you do that? Can you be a
          volunteer FBI agent?

                    EARL, A PRODUCER
          Montana didn't give us much choice
          in the matter. He said if we didn't
          help him get them, for what they'd
          done to his brother, he'd get his
          own revenge. Thanks to Montana,
          this whole case has come together.

                    SHIRLEY/WAITRESS
          But the parking lot, that
          explosion. What was that?

Montana goes silent, looks at Earl.

                    EARL, A PRODUCER
          That was an FBI agent, named
          Jefferson. I suspected Santiago was
          up to something but I couldn't find
          out what he had planned. Special
          agent Mike Jefferson doubled for
          Montana.

                    MONTANA
                (sudden anger)
          I didn't want him to do that. I
          told you I could handle it.

                    EARL, A PRODUCER
          I've got a supervisor. It was his
          decision. I take orders. You agreed
          to take orders, too.

                    SHIRLEY/WAITRESS
          Is that what you two were arguing
          about, backstage, after the show?

                    EARL, A PRODUCER
          Yes. Agent Jefferson would have
          been covered from someone who we
          had an ID for.
                    (MORE)

                    EARL, A PRODUCER (CONT'D)
          But we didn't expect a stranger, a
          suicidal religious nut, he came
          from nowhere. Jefferson walked
          right in to him.

Shirley sits, looking back and forth, from Earl to Montana.
Back to Montana.

                    SHIRLEY/WAITRESS
          So.
               (beat)
          What happens next?

                    MONTANA
               (beat)
          That's a good question.

                                        FADE TO BLACK.

The author draws upon the mysteries of the past and the ambiguities and "alternative facts" of the present for inspiration. His research into current and historical events delves into the specifics and the speculations, approached, and perceived, from his skeptic's point of view.

He is keen to expose the satirical elements of the human condition, from whoever and wherever they may be found. He is a big fan of tall tales told around the campfire of the drama and the slapstick of the ancient and continuing story of *Homo sapiens*. He wonders about our ancestors, how they became us, and what we, in turn, shall evolve to come to be.

Question: What happenings, from the history of our times, will inspire that future version of *Homo sapiens* to create their own tall tales; and how will we, as the characters in their stories, be visualized? Furthermore, will they have evolved to become more rational creatures; or will they, like us, be susceptible to "alternative facts", fearful of superstition, and be willing subjects to mind-bending propaganda?

➤ The screenplay, *10,000 COMEDIANS – the no BS! tour*, combines the allure of Hollywood and a rodeo cowboy's career change to stand up comedy, with the hard reality of international crime and corruption. It also explores the definition and consequences of humor; that is, how does comedy, a joke, that is funny to one person, become an insult and an existential crisis to another person.

➤ The screenplay and stage play, *What's Your Disorder? the Reality Show,* is live theatre, where the audience and the actors participate in an interactive experience. Each group understands the circumstances differently, leading to a misinterpretation of intention with catastrophic results.

➤ The screenplay, *NORTHSTAR*, offers an imagined yet very plausible scenario to what may have happened to the $9 BILLION dollars cash that unaccountably went missing during the 2003 invasion of Iraq.

➤ The novel of historical fiction and the screenplay adaptation, *The Lost Gospels of Mariam and Judas*, is a secular, rational, non-supernatural, alternative version of the story of the 1st-century Galilean man, Yeshua the Nazarene.

➤ The novel, *Will it Play in Peoria, The Autobiography of the Reverend William Williams*, is a retrospective view of the tumultuous 1960's Hippies and Yippies, and the sex, drugs, rock & roll, peace, love, war, harmony, and rage, that defined the era.